"Turn around and let me see your butt."

Sam knew that snakes were in deep hibernation at this time of year. But if Sarah thought she'd been bitten, it was his duty to investigate.

"This is the ultimate humiliation. I think I'd prefer to die from the poison," Sarah said, reluctantly tugging her jeans down.

Sam ran his hand over the gentle curve of her hip. He couldn't see a single mark. "I suppose it could be a snakebite. Maybe I should suck out the venom."

"Don't you dare!" Sarah cried.

"Snake poison can be deadly," he reminded her.

She sighed, shaking her head. "All right. Go ahead."

God, it was fun to mess with her. "Hold still." Softly Sam pressed his mouth to her hip, then touched her skin with his tongue.

Sarah turned around, regarding him suspiciously. "I wasn't bitten by a snake, was I?"

He smiled. "No. But I'm sure enjoying the view."

Dear Reader,

It's very difficult to know what to say. For eleven years Harlequin Temptation has been my home. I've written over forty books for this series, and now this one is my last.

I remember my first book so well—*Indecent Exposure.* It seems like just yesterday that I got the call from Harlequin, telling me they were interested in publishing my manuscript. And since then I've had the privilege of creating many stories to share with you.

I hope you'll continue to look for my books under the Harlequin imprint. The Mighty Quinns will be back in February with my first family saga, *The Promise.* And then I'll be making the move to Harlequin Blaze, where you'll find the rest of the Quinn family in 2006.

For now, though, I hope you enjoy *Warm & Willing.* And visit my Web site at www.katehoffmann.com for all the news about my upcoming releases.

Best wishes,

Kate Hoffmann

Books by Kate Hoffmann

KATE HOFFMANN
Warm & Willing

 HARLEQUIN®

TORONTO • NEW YORK • LONDON
AMSTERDAM • PARIS • SYDNEY • HAMBURG
STOCKHOLM • ATHENS • TOKYO • MILAN • MADRID
PRAGUE • WARSAW • BUDAPEST • AUCKLAND

To my editors at Harlequin Temptation, who've provided
inspiration and support over the past eleven years.
And to my readers, who've been with me from the
first Temptation novel to the last. This one's for you!

ISBN 0-373-69217-X

WARM & WILLING

Copyright © 2005 by Peggy A. Hoffmann.

1

HE FELT HER WARMTH before he even touched her. The room was dark, so black he couldn't rely on his sense of sight. She lay beside him in the bed, the warm curve of her backside nestled into his lap. Sam hesitated before he touched her, certain that she was just a figment of his imagination, another dream that would be snatched away before he could find satisfaction.

But when he reached for her, she sighed and whispered his name. It had been such a long time, Sam wondered how he'd be able to take it slow. His body ached with the need for release, yet he didn't want to rush. He craved the sweet torture that came with losing himself deep inside a woman.

He drew a breath and then smoothed his hand over her naked belly. Her skin was like silk, so warm and soft beneath his callused fingers. He gently turned her in his arms, finding her lips and kissing her softly. She responded immediately, opening to his gentle assault.

The kiss was intoxicating, like a glass of warmed brandy on a cold night. That warmth seeped though his bloodstream, propelled by the slow, even pulse of his heart. He didn't know who she was or where she'd come from, but he wanted her all the same.

"Touch me," he murmured, guiding her hand to

his body. Her fingers danced over his skin, teasing at the hair on his belly before dropping lower. He held his breath, waiting for the rush of heat when she wrapped her fingers around him and began to stroke his shaft.

A low moan rumbled in his throat as he gave himself over to the intense sensations coursing through his body. He was close, his release just a heartbeat away. Still, he held back. But as red-hot desire swirled within him, he felt himself losing the battle for control.

And then, suddenly, she stopped. "What's wrong?" he whispered, his question laced with desperation.

"Is there a donut shop on the corner or will I have to go to the airport?"

Slowly, Sam found his way back from the brink and opened his eyes. He still couldn't see her, but he knew she'd never been there at all. Gulping in a deep breath, he sat up and glanced around the dimly lit interior of the cabin. "Donut shop?" he murmured, raking his fingers through his hair. "What the hell?"

Embers still glowed in the fireplace and as his vision cleared, he realized he'd been dreaming again. He cursed at the bizarre and decidedly unsatisfying end to his dream, then flopped back on the bed, his skin slick with sweat.

"It's time to get out of here," he murmured, wincing at the unresolved ache in his groin.

Light filtered through the small windows, telling him it was well past dawn. He'd tidy up the cabin, pack his things, and in a few hours, hike back to the civilized world. And once he'd reached Sutter Gap, he'd find a warm and willing woman, one who wouldn't evaporate before he had a chance to come.

Sam crawled off the bed and walked to the rough plank door. He threw it open and let the cold air hit his naked body, blasting away the last traces of his dream. The sky above the leafless trees was clear and blue, forecasting good weather for his trip.

Spring had come to his little corner of the Appalachian wilderness two weeks ago, the rising temperatures melting the dense cover of snow in the higher elevations of the Blue Ridge Mountains. He'd thought about making the hike out a few days before, but a driving rain had changed his mind. In good weather, it took a long day's walk to reach the little town of Sutter Gap, but if he had to slog through swollen streams and ankle-deep mud, the hike could take two.

Sam went back inside the cabin and tossed another log on the fire, poking at the embers. He'd run out of coffee last month and had been existing on the last of the beans and rice for the past week. The thought of a thick, juicy steak and a baked potato made his mouth water.

Strange how a man's needs could be reduced to just two things—sex and red meat. And a hot shower, maybe. If he could find a way to enjoy all three at the same time, then he wouldn't have to choose which to pursue first.

He'd lived a monkish life for the past six months, a simple existence in a rough log cabin, perched on a mountainside among the thick forests of western North Carolina. Over the past three years, the cabin had become home.

Sam smiled as he remembered his first winter living in the woods. He'd craved sex and Snickers candy bars. And when he'd returned to civilization, he'd eaten twenty candy bars in two days and spent a week in bed with a pretty bartender from a road-house outside of Asheville.

During his second winter it was sex and the music of Linkin Park. After he'd gotten back, he'd driven around for over a week with their latest CD in his disc player and spent his nights with a sexy nature guide from Smokey Mountains National Park.

Sam wondered just what kind of woman would share his bed this time around. It was always a bit tricky, explaining his situation and his particular needs to a potential bedmate. Most single women were interested in a romantic relationship, one that might result in marriage. Sam's only interest was in a wildly exciting, no-strings attached sexual encounter lasting approximately one week.

To his surprise, he'd found quite a few women who required nothing more than unbridled passion with a skilled and eager partner. After a week together, there was nothing more to experience and both parties went away well satisfied.

Sam grabbed a pair of faded jeans from the hook on the wall and tugged them on. He'd first walked into the mountains a few months after the death of his best friend, Jeff Warren. They'd climbed Mt. McKinley together and on the way down, Jeff had been swept away in an avalanche, gone in an instant, buried deep beneath the snow.

Adventure had become almost an obsession for the two of them. Every extra dime they'd made from their jobs on Wall Street had been spent searching for bigger and better thrills. And when Sam had suggested a climb up McKinley, Jeff had barely been able to contain his enthusiasm. It had all been good, the crazy thrill of standing on top of one of the world's seven summits. And then it had suddenly turned so bad. In a heartbeat, Jeff was dead and Sam had been left to rue the day he'd ever mentioned Mt. McKinley.

The first book Sam had read after the funeral had been Thoreau's *Walden Pond* and he'd gotten from it the idea of living a quieter, simpler life, what he hoped would be a remedy for his chaotic emotions. So he'd quit his job and set out on his most challenging adventure—to spend a winter in the wilderness, completely alone.

Luckily, that first winter had been mild. He'd come with just a tent, a warm sleeping bag, some rudimentary tools and a book about wilderness survival. He'd camped on a piece of privately owned, inheld land, surrounded by national forest and set on top of a small mountain range.

In his determination to live off the land, Sam had nearly starved. He'd decided not to bring a gun for hunting and was left to fashion snares out of vines and saplings. He had quickly exhausted his taste for wild roots and edible plants and the occasional rabbit that wandered into his snare, yet he'd refused to give up.

He'd left his camp that spring knowing he'd become a different man on those long, lonely winter nights—a man he could look at in the mirror again. A man who could face anything life threw at him.

Over the following summer, he'd prepared to go back to his former life, but when autumn had rolled around, Sam had packed more tools and spent the winter working on a rough log cabin. It had been slow progress all alone, but by the time spring had come, he'd had a cozy shelter with a stone fireplace and a roof over his head.

He'd begun recording his experiences and thoughts in a small diary as a way to pass his evenings. And when he'd hiked out after his second winter, Sam had decided to submit a few of his stories to an adventure magazine. The editor had been impressed and scheduled the stories to run in a regular column starting that October. But by October, Sam was back in the wilderness again.

He filled his days with finding food and chopping firewood and making improvements to the cabin. The long winter nights were a time to contemplate the man he'd been and the man he'd become. But there was a limit to his need for solitude and he'd passed it about a month ago.

Sam grabbed the water bucket and walked out the front door of the cabin. He followed the well-worn path to a small stream that carried runoff from high in the mountains. It was nice not to have to melt snow to bathe and shave. He wondered what it would take to dig a well on his mountainside.

As he walked back up to the cabin, Sam was startled to see a lone figure waiting on the front steps. He hadn't seen another person for months. But when the man turned, Sam chuckled and shook his head. "Carter Wilbury! What are you doing on my mountain?"

The elderly man waved and dropped his pack beside him. "Sam Morgan! If I remember correctly, I own this mountain and pretty much all the land around it."

"I was just on my way down," Sam said when he joined the older man. "How was your hike up?"

"Not bad. Took a while for me to work the winter

'out of my bones. Could have done the whole thing in a day, but I camped down below last night. Just couldn't work up the energy to climb this last bit. I thought you might see my campfire and walk down to investigate."

Though Sam considered himself a competent outdoorsman, Carter Wilbury was a real mountain man. Carter had once broken his leg in a twenty-foot tumble off a rock ledge, then crawled for six days to get help. He'd eaten bugs and grubs and worms and drunk the dew off leaves to stay alive. Since then, he'd been a legend around Sutter Gap. But age and a bad bout of frostbite had kept Carter indoors in the winter—that and a pretty widow who had captured his fancy.

Sam picked up the man's pack and dragged it through the front door. "I'd offer you a cup of coffee, but I ran out a few weeks back."

"I brought some along," Carter said, bending down to rummage through his pack. "Just show me where the pot is."

Sam grabbed the pot from the dry sink and filled it with water from the pitcher. "So what brings you up here so early in the season?"

"Came here to warn ya," Carter said.

Sam froze. "About what?"

"There's a woman nosing around Sutter Gap. She found out you like to frequent the Lucky Penny when you're in town and she's waiting for you to come back."

"Who is she?" Sam asked.

Carter shrugged. "Says her name is Sarah Cantrell. She won't say what she wants, but she's a persistent little thing. She tried to pay me five hundred dollars to bring her up here, but I told her I didn't know where you were."

"What did she look like?"

"Pretty. Real pretty. City girl. Nice fingernails, fancy makeup and she wears the damnedest boots with these funny little heels. And she's always messing with her cell phone. Most of the boys at the bar have been drooling over her but all she's interested in is you." Carter paused. "I saw that *Fatal Attraction* movie on HBO a few months back. You don't think she's…"

"A bunny boiler?"

"No, got a Sam Jr. she wants to show you. You are quite the ladies' man when you're off this mountain."

"Did she have a baby with her?"

"No, but do the math. You came off the mountain in April of last year. It's late March now. She could have photos of a two-month-old to show you."

"Listen, I may enjoy the company of women, but I do it responsibly."

Carter nodded. "Well, then, I guess we can rule out the social diseases as well. Maybe a relative died and she's here to tell you you've inherited a fortune. Or maybe she's one of those reporters looking to do a story on a modern-day Daniel Boone."

Sam considered the possibilities for a moment, then shrugged. "I suppose I'll know soon enough. Thanks for watching my back."

"No problem," Carter said.

Sam considered the ramifications of Carter's news. "Can you do it again? Watch my back, I mean. When we get back to Sutter Gap, I want you to tell this woman you know someone who can take her to see Sam Morgan."

"Who? Besides you and me, no one else knows how to get up here. And you know how the folks are in Sutter Gap. They don't talk to strangers."

"Just introduce her to me, your cousin. Call me... Charlie Wilbury, your friendly, neighborhood wilderness guide. And give everyone at the Lucky Penny the heads-up. I'll just tell her I'm going to take her to Sam Morgan and in turn, she'll tell me what she wants."

"So you think she's trouble?"

"I don't know," Sam said. "But it won't take me more than a few minutes to find out."

"I CAN'T BELIEVE I've spent ten whole days in this backwater town with nothing to show for it," Sarah Cantrell muttered. She glanced over her shoulder at the patrons of the Lucky Penny tavern then turned back to the old pay phone, feeling their eyes boring into her back.

The town of Sutter Gap, population two hundred, sat nestled in the mountain country of North Carolina, just a few miles from the Tennessee border. The main street boasted just two businesses—a tiny grocery store which also served as the town gas station, the post office and the bait shop; and the Lucky Penny Tavern. The rest of the town was made up of a hodge-podge of houses, cobbled together without regard for architectural style. Sarah had taken a room at the Gap View Motor Lodge just out of town, a place that usually housed visiting hunters.

"I'm a nice southern girl, but this is not the south," she continued. "If I'm not careful, one of these good old boys is going to toss me in the back of his pickup, take me to his cabin in the woods and chain me to the bed."

"You're a beautiful woman and men are bound to look," Libby Marbury said, her voice crackling back over the phone line. "They're probably just lonesome."

Libby Parrish Marbury had been Sarah's best friend since they were in seventh grade. Over the years, they'd given each other endless advice on men and romance. But there was no way even Libby could put a positive spin on the social prospects in Sutter Gap, North Carolina.

"They don't just look," Sarah complained. "They grunt and leer and a few of them drool. I know I've complained about the dating scene in Belfort, but I feel like I've landed on another planet here. A planet where ragged flannel and faded denim is the height of fashion and a good catch is a man who can bring down a ten-point buck with his bare hands. The odds are pretty good here, but the goods are definitely odd."

"You're not there to find a man," Libby insisted. "At least, not in the romantic sense, so why let it bother you?"

"It doesn't bother me," Sarah said. "I'm just a little frustrated with the waiting."

For such a long time, she and Libby had been in the same boat—single and searching for love. But since Libby's wedding, Sarah had become acutely aware of the differences between them. Libby had always taken a very cautious approach to love, waiting patiently for her Prince Charming to sweep her off her feet, knowing that some day he'd come.

Sarah had always preferred a more adventurous attitude toward men, juggling several different boyfriends at once and then discarding them when they became too demanding or too troublesome. In truth, she didn't want love at all, just fire and heat and passion. Libby had once quipped that Sarah took a "catch and release" approach to the men in her life. Men were like fish, once she'd caught them, it was only a matter of time before she tossed them back.

"I've turned down three invitations since I got to town," Sarah continued. "One guy wanted me to go coon hunting, and one offered an evening of bowling in Asheville. The other cut right to the chase. He wanted to take me home to meet his mama."

"Do you really expect Sam Morgan to be any different?" Libby asked.

"I sure hope he is. It would take me a whole lot more than I've got budgeted to turn any of these guys into a television personality."

"How long are you going to wait for this guy?" Libby asked.

"I don't know. This is the biggest get of my career. Sam Morgan has been living in the wilderness for three years, all alone. He survives on nuts and berries. He built a log cabin with his own two hands. He's PBS gold. Imagine the potential. The program would be part reality television, part adventure and travel and part educational. Plus, we've got the whole pioneer history thing going. If he's halfway presentable, the show could be a huge hit."

"And if he isn't?"

"At least his name sounds rugged. I'm hoping he looks like a cross between Robert Redford and the Marlboro man. We need to attract female viewers as well as male. If he's missing all his teeth I don't know what I'll do."

"What if Mr. Morgan doesn't want you nosing around his life?"

"Well, he obviously wants some sort of recognition or he wouldn't have written those articles for *Outdoor Adventure*. I just hope I can get to him before the network guys do. Those reality show producers are always on the prowl for the next big idea and they can offer him a lot more money than I can. But all they're interested in is ratings and drama. I'd do this right."

"You're a very persuasive woman when you want to be," Libby said. "I'm sure you'll be able to get this guy to agree to your idea."

"I hope so."

It had been sheer luck that she'd stumbled across Sam Morgan. Two months ago, she'd been in the dentist's office and had picked up an issue of *Outdoor Adventure*. After reading Sam Morgan's article, she'd cancelled her appointment, gone back to the station and had immediately begun preparing a pitch for a new PBS series called *Wilderness*.

It was the perfect next step in her career. She'd begun work at the PBS affiliate in Charleston eight years earlier, as a twenty-two-year-old production assistant. She'd worked her way up to producer at WCLC, but when she'd first proposed the idea for Libby's cooking show, of *Southern Comforts*, it was with the idea of striking out on her own. She'd quit her job and formed her own production company and before long, she and Libby had put together the funding to produce *Southern Comforts*.

They'd never expected the show to be such a resounding hit. *Southern Comforts* was now the jewel in WCLC's programming crown, seen in nearly one hundred PBS markets nationwide. And from the moment she'd finished production on the second season, the station had begun clamoring for another new show.

Wilderness would be that show. And once it was a success, the production company she'd founded three years ago would finally be on firm footing. She could pay back the business loan she'd taken and maybe even give herself a small salary raise as well.

"If I can just find him, I'm sure I can convince him," Sarah said.

"So what else do you know about Sam Morgan?" Libby asked.

"Nothing. No one in town is talking. This old guy named Carter Wilbury is supposed to be his friend, but he won't—" Sarah felt a tap on her shoulder. She held up her hand. "I'll be through in a sec."

"What?" Libby asked.

"Someone wants to use the phone," Sarah replied, annoyed with the interruption. "So, tell me, how are you feeling? Has the morning sickness gotten any better?"

"I'm much better. Trey brings me crackers in bed and I've found that regular servings of Rocky Road ice cream seem to settle my stomach. And my clothes are starting to get really tight, though I'm not sure if that's from the baby or all the ice cream."

Sarah pulled her BlackBerry PDA out of her purse and scanned her calendar. "I'll be back home next week at the latest. We can go shopping at that cute little maternity shop on—" Sarah felt another tap on her shoulder. She spun around, angry at the second rude interruption. "I said I'd be done in—"

The words froze in her throat as she came face-to-face with the most beautiful man in all of Sutter Gap—and probably in the entire state of North Carolina as well. Sarah coughed to hide her surprise. "I—I'm sorry. I'll just get off now." She reached back to hang up the phone, but missed the hook twice.

"I understand you're looking for Sam Morgan," he said.

Sarah stared into his eyes, deep blue and ringed with impossibly long, dark lashes. "I—um, I'll be—"

Libby's voice came over the phone. "Sarah? Are you still there?"

Shaken from her stupor, Sarah turned back to face the wall and whispered into the phone. "Lib, I have to go."

"Is everything all right?"

She cupped her hand over the receiver. "I might have been completely wrong about the men in Sutter Gap."

"What?"

"I'll call you later with the details." With that, she quickly hung up the phone and spun back around, smoothing her hair and gracing him with a bright smile. She held out her hand. "Hello there, I'm Sarah Cantrell."

The man stared down at her outstretched fingers, examining her manicure for a long moment before taking her hand in his callused palm. "Charlie Wilbury," he muttered, his thumb brushing across the back of her wrist.

"Wilbury?" she asked. "Are you related to Carter Wilbury? Or Hattie Wilbury who runs the Gap View Motor Lodge?"

"Probably," he replied.

Though he was dressed like all the others at the Lucky Penny, this man managed to make scruffy look incredibly sexy. His features were close to perfection, the sculpted mouth and the chiseled jaw, the blue eyes that seemed to see right into her soul. Even the dark stubble of beard that shadowed his strong jaw was attractive on him, while the same unshaven look came across as untidy on the rest of the patrons of the bar.

Millions of questions raced through her mind. What was a man like him doing in a place like this? Was this all some altitude-induced hallucination, or was he real? And why was he wearing so damn many clothes? Why was she wearing so many clothes? Suddenly, the room seemed very warm.

Sarah gulped back her silly questions and forced a smile. "Do you know Sam Morgan?"

"I do," Charlie said, his gaze now fixed on her face.

Sarah groaned inwardly as a tiny grin twitched at the corners of his mouth. Maybe he *could* read her mind. She quickly tried to dispel the image of a naked mountain man from her head.

"And what do you need with Sam?"

Sarah shifted as his eyes now focused on her lips. Good grief, the way he was smiling at her was quite unnerving, as if he were seriously contemplating ravishing her right there in the bar. "I need to talk to him."

"About what?"

His blunt question took her by surprise and she tried to regain control of her senses. "Well, that's really none of your business."

Charlie chuckled and let go of her hand. "No, I suppose it isn't. But you're the one looking for him, lady, not me."

He turned, sauntered over to the bar and sat down on a bar stool.

She studied him from a distance. He wore faded jeans that hugged his long legs and a canvas jacket that looked like he'd recently used it for a doormat. The soft flannel shirt beneath his jacket was open just enough to reveal a smooth chest. His hiking boots were scuffed and his dark hair was just a little too long, curling over the collar of his jacket.

He was not prone to gaping at her, which set him apart from the rabble nursing their beers, munching on peanuts and debating the nutritional value of beef jerky.

A shiver skittered down her spine as she imagined what it might be like to unbutton his shirt, to run her hands over his chest and to press her lips to his skin. There was something about all that rugged masculinity wrapped up in denim and flannel that left her just a little dizzy. She moaned softly. This was neither the time nor the place for erotic musings!

Sarah drew a deep breath and started toward him. Right now, Charlie Wilbury was her only way to Sam Morgan. And Sam Morgan was her only way to another successful show. If she had to use every last ounce of her sex appeal to get what she wanted from Mr. Wilbury, then she would. But it would be strictly a business tactic. Sarah slipped onto the bar stool next to him. "Can I buy you a drink, Mr. Wilbury?"

"Depends on what you expect in return," he said. "If you expect me to get all sloppy drunk so you can take advantage of me, then yes, you can buy me several drinks."

Sarah smiled. She hadn't expected to encounter both unique wit and simmering masculinity here in Sutter Gap. It was highly enjoyable. And given the choice, she could think of whole list of things she would also enjoy, beginning with a slow striptease and ending with a night of passion in her motel room…if she were living in Sarah Cantrell's Sexual Fantasyland where every handsome man was interested in pleasuring her. But she wasn't.

"You said you know Sam Morgan. Do you know where he is right now?"

Charlie nodded. "I do."

Sarah opened her purse and withdrew a twenty, placing it on the bar. The bartender poured Charlie a whiskey straight up and left the bottle. Sarah ordered a diet cola, deciding it would be better to keep her head together than impress him with her drinking abilities. "Could you take me to him?"

"Sam's a real private person. He doesn't like strangers, even if they do look like you."

There was a compliment in there somewhere. "Surprise, surprise," she murmured. "*No one* in this town likes strangers. And no one knows anything about Sam Morgan either."

"Or maybe they just don't want to talk to you."

"This is very important," Sarah said, reaching out to touch his hand. The moment she did, she had cause to regret her action. A strange tingle numbed her fingers and began to climb up her arm. "I—I have a business proposal for him that could be financially beneficial. I think it's only fair that he make his own decision about this."

Charlie set down his whiskey glass and ran his thumb back and forth over the back of her hand. "And what makes you think Sam is interested in money?"

"Everyone is interested in money," Sarah said. Although, right now, all she was interested in was the strange effect Charlie Wilbury's touch was having on her body.

He downed the rest of his whiskey and set the glass on the bar, then slowly stood. "Not everyone, Ms. Cantrell. Hell, I'm interested in lots of other things besides money." He let his gaze skim lazily up and down her body. "You probably are, too, right?" With that, he started toward the door.

Sarah gasped. Just what was he intimating? Yes, she was attracted to him. And the thought of tearing his clothes off and having her way with him had crossed her mind—once, twice at the most. But she certainly could set aside basic lust in order to focus on the real reason she'd come to Sutter Gap.

She grabbed her purse and ran, catching up to him on the sidewalk outside the bar. "Wait!" He stopped and she circled around him, preventing him from taking another step. "I'll pay you five hundred dollars if you get me a meeting with Sam Morgan."

"You still haven't told me what you want."

Sarah stared up at him, losing herself in his gaze for a long moment. He had the most mesmerizing blue eyes. Suddenly all thoughts of business fled from her head. If she told him what she really wanted from him, what would he do? What a silly question! From the way he was looking at her, he wasn't the kind of man who waited for an engraved invitation.

"One thousand dollars," she said in a shaky voice, knowing that she'd wipe out the last of her checking account to get what she wanted. "You take me to Sam Morgan, no questions asked." But after she made the offer, Sarah wondered if she could trust the man behind those eyes. Could she trust any man who made her heart flutter and her pulse pound, a man who looked as if he were ready to toss her against the nearest car and have his way with her?

"Nope," he said. He started off again, but she grabbed his arm.

"All right. Here's the deal. I want to make a television show about Sam Morgan's experiences in the wilderness. I own a small production company and we work with the PBS station in Charleston, South Carolina. It would be a multimedia deal. There'd be a companion book, speaking engagements, special appearances. I've read Mr. Morgan's articles in *Outdoor Adventure* and he's a wonderful writer. I can make him famous."

Charlie laughed out loud. "Famous?"

"As famous as...Bob Vila. Or Julia Child."

"So you like his writing?" Charlie asked. "I always thought his prose was a little flowery."

"Not at all," Sarah protested. "It's descriptive and evocative. He has such a wonderful way with detail, yet there's an innate simplicity to his words. Do you know if he's an educated man?"

Charlie hesitated, as if contemplating how much he was willing to reveal. "I'd say he's just about the smartest guy I've ever met. I'd even call him brilliant. But he's also very humble."

"And what about his dental situation," she asked. "Does he have all his teeth?"

Sam's eyebrow shot up. "Yes, I believe he does."

Sarah sighed in relief. She was finally getting somewhere. But she still had to convince Charlie Wilbury to take her to Sam. "I could really use your help. Maybe we could have dinner tonight and I could explain all the details."

She swallowed hard, wondering if the invitation sounded too desperate. But she *was* desperate—to find Sam Morgan. And maybe a tiny bit interested in his friend Charlie Wilbury. "I'm sure Mr. Morgan will want to listen to my proposal, but I'll let you be the judge."

"Where are you staying?"

"At the Gap View Motor Lodge out on Route 18. Room nine."

He studied her for a long moment, then shrugged. "All right. I'll pick you up at seven. Dress warmly," he said. With that, Charlie Wilbury walked down the street, whistling softly, his hands shoved in the pockets of his jacket.

Sarah watched him go, staring at his backside and admiring the view. She shivered again, then rubbed her arms through her wool jacket. It had been a long time since she'd found a man so devastatingly attractive. And had he been just an ordinary man, she might have considered seducing him.

But it had always been her policy never to mix business with pleasure. She sighed. "A guy like Charlie Wilbury would be a good reason to revise that policy," she murmured.

SAM STARED at his reflection in the rearview mirror, then raked his hands through his hair. Maybe he should have taken more care with his appearance. After all, this was a date of sorts. He was taking a beautiful woman to dinner, the closest thing he'd had to a real social engagement in almost three years.

"What the hell am I doing?" he muttered.

It had been a simple plan—hide his identity, find out what she wanted and then get the hell out of town. But now that he knew exactly what she wanted, why was he still hanging around? He had no intention of agreeing to her proposal.

Obviously he was staying because Sarah Cantrell made his pulse race and his blood warm. From the moment he'd met her, he'd thought about nothing but getting her into bed. For a man who'd done without sex for months, that wasn't unexpected. But his fantasies were strangely detailed, imagining the feel of her breast in his hand or the warmth of her mouth on his skin or the—

Sam cursed softly. Nothing good could come of his deception. If he had any intention of inviting her into his bed, then he needed to tell her the truth as soon as possible. Sam tipped his head back and groaned. Why couldn't he have stumbled across a less complicated woman? Usually when he came down from the cabin, he found himself a woman with exactly the same wants and needs that he had—great sex and lots of it. So why was he even considering seducing Sarah Cantrell?

"She's beautiful, for one," he murmured. With a body any man would want to put his hands on. But there was more to it than just a physical attraction. Sarah Cantrell was smart and funny and stubborn and resourceful, the kind of woman who'd probably make seduction a challenge.

And women like Sarah didn't just drop out of the sky every day, especially in Sutter Gap. If his instincts were right, and they usually were when it came to the opposite sex, she wanted him as much as he wanted her. So what was stopping him?

Carter had called her a pretty little thing. The old guy always did have a knack for understatement.

There was something about the auburn hair and the perfect skin and the lush mouth that made him believe Sarah Cantrell might just be the most gorgeous, intriguing woman he'd ever met.

The thought of slowly undressing her, of running his hands over her naked body and touching her in her most intimate spots, made his pulse pound. "Right now, any woman would look good," he reminded himself.

Sam turned off the ignition and hopped out of the SUV. "Just tell her who you are," he said as he strode up to room number nine, "turn down her proposal and go from there."

He rapped on the door, then stood back. Though this wasn't a date, it sure felt like one. He was already cataloguing topics he might call upon if the conversation dwindled and she seemed bored.

A few seconds later, Sarah pulled open the door. Sam's breath caught in his throat as the light from the room lit her from behind. Her hair tumbled in soft waves around her face. She wore a pale green sweater that clung to her body like a second skin, molding to the curves of her breasts. The neckline scooped low in the front, revealing just a tiny bit of cleavage.

Sam swallowed hard. Why did there have to be cleavage? Now he'd spend the rest of the night thinking about pressing his lips to that very spot on her body. "Hi," he murmured.

"I'll just be a second," Sarah said, gracing him with a warm smile.

Sam watched her from the doorway as she gathered her jacket and purse from the bed. She wore a wool skirt that hugged her backside and revealed the tantalizing length of her legs. Black leather boots hugged her calves and an image of those legs wrapped around his waist flashed in his head. He'd forgotten just how arousing a woman's body could be when fully clothed.

When she turned around, he was caught staring. He cleared his throat. Now was the time to come clean and tell her the truth. But then again, he didn't want to spend the entire evening talking business. He'd wait until after dinner. "Ready?"

Sam stepped aside as she walked out, then he hurried to open the door to his SUV. When she was settled in her seat, he closed the door and circled around the front of the truck. After three years of living in the wild, he was almost surprised he remembered basic etiquette.

As he steered the truck out of town, Sam turned his attention to the sharply winding road. The lights from the SUV illuminated the trees and they headed deeper into the woods. He stole a quick glace at Sarah and saw a worried frown wrinkling her brow.

"You're going to love this place," Sam assured her. "The view is incredible. And the food is great."

"How does a restaurant survive so far out in the sticks?" Sarah asked in an uneasy tone.

"It has a very exclusive clientele," he explained.

"I—I think I'd prefer to eat a little bit closer to town."

He pulled off the county road and carefully maneuvered the truck down a narrow dirt drive, the path marked by two ruts cut through the woods. As they bumped along, Sarah clutched the dashboard, her eyes wide. "Where are you taking me?"

Sam heard the concern in her voice and figured her mind was beginning to form images of serial killers and axe murderers. Just how far was she willing to go to find Sam Morgan? She'd already driven into the woods with a virtual stranger. Would she sleep with a wilderness guide who promised to take her to Morgan? "We're almost there," he said.

Sam slowly pulled the truck to a stop in a small clearing, then turned off the ignition. He jumped out of the truck and circled around to her side to open the door. But she quickly locked all the doors. "I'm not getting out," she shouted through the window, fear lacing her words. "I don't like it here."

Sam held up the keyless remote and pushed the button to unlock the doors. But Sarah quickly locked them all again from the inside. Sam chuckled. "You're willing to let me take you to Sam Morgan but you're not willing to eat dinner with me?"

"How do know that you're not some—some—"

"Look in the bag on the back seat," Sam said. "You'll find two steaks, a couple of potatoes, and a bottle of wine. We're going to be dining al fresco tonight. There's a nice spot just down the trail."

She crawled over the seat and rummaged through the grocery bag. A few moments later, she opened the door, an apologetic expression on her face. Holding out his hand, he helped her down. But he didn't let go of her fingers, determined to touch her for as long as he wanted. "Don't worry," he murmured, bending so close that his lips nearly brushed her cheek. "You'll be perfectly safe with me."

"I don't know many psychos who know what al fresco means," she muttered. "So I guess I'm safe. But where are we?"

Sam opened the rear door and grabbed a flashlight then handed it to her. "The best spot in Sutter

Gap." After finding a flashlight for himself, he grabbed the grocery bag. Then he took her hand and pulled her along with him on a narrow trail. When she stumbled slightly, he stopped and slipped his arm around her waist. "Are you all right?"

"These boots really weren't made for wandering around in the woods," Sarah explained.

"Then you're going to need a new pair of boots," he replied.

"Does that mean you're going to take me to see Sam Morgan?"

"I haven't decided yet," Sam said. Hell, he didn't know what he was doing. Right now, this whole evening was a fly-by-the-seat-of-his-pants affair.

They continued to walk, Sarah stumbling around beside him and cursing softly. When they reached the end of the path, Sam set the grocery bag on a rough plank table set next to a fire ring. "Come on, I want to show you something."

He took her hand again, the mere contact sending a current through his fingers. He helped her navigate around the huge slabs of stone to the edge of the gap. As they stepped from the cover of the woods, the entire valley spread out in front of them, lights twinkling from distant towns and small cabins scattered throughout the mountains.

He waited, curious as to how she'd react. For some reason, Sam wanted her to understand what had brought him to the wilderness—this perfect isolation and breathtaking beauty. Maybe then she'd understand why he couldn't accept her proposal.

"Oh," she murmured, her voice filled with awe. "Look at this. You can see forever."

The full moon hung low on the horizon, casting a

soft light over the valley below. It was perfect, he thought. It had never looked more scenic. He'd never shared this view with anyone, but it seemed right to show it to her.

"Where are we?" she asked.

"My place," Sam said. "Or it will be someday. Right now, it's just my little piece of land. My trees, my rocks, my view. I stay out here sometimes when I'm in town."

"Where do you sleep?" Sarah said, glancing around.

"I pitch a tent. It's a perfect spot."

She nodded, looking back out at the valley. "The world seems so much bigger from this vantage point. It makes me feel very small...and insignificant." She laughed softly. "I have to admit, I was a little frightened coming out here with you. I was wondering if I'd made a mistake. But now I see I haven't."

He looked over at her, the urge to kiss her overwhelming. After slipping his arm around her waist, he slowly urged her closer. The beams from their flashlights wavered in the trees. He couldn't see her reaction, but she didn't try to pull away.

"I think I understand why you brought me here," she murmured.

Sam let his flashlight fall to the ground, then reached out and touched her face, spreading his fingers across her cheeks. His mind went back to the dream he'd had that last night in his cabin, to the woman who'd seduced him in his sleep.

"I have my reasons," Sam whispered.

At first, he fought the impulse to kiss Sarah. But then his curiosity got the better of him. Could Sarah Cantrell be that woman for him? He pulled her into a kiss, his mouth finding hers in the dark. A tiny sigh of surprise slipped from her lips and she dropped her flashlight next to his.

The instant she did, she opened herself to the kiss, her tongue teasing at his, inviting him to take more. She tasted sweet, and like a man parched with thirst, he was desperate to drink his fill. When he finally drew back, he could almost see the profile of her face in the moonlight.

"That wasn't the reason I expected," Sarah whispered. "But I guess it will do."

He nuzzled her neck. "What?"

"Why you brought me here," she said, tilting her head.

Sam brushed another kiss across her lips, satisfied that the first step in his seduction had gone well. "I brought you here for dinner. I just skipped ahead to dessert."

She bent down and picked up her flashlight, then shined it in his eyes. "And what about the main course? Are you going to cook for me?"

He turned the flashlight on her face. "Nope. I thought you could cook for me," Sam said.

He waited for her to protest but she just shook her head. "I sense this is a test. If I don't do well, then you're not going to take me to meet Sam Morgan."

Maybe now was the time to come clean, Sam thought. He'd kissed her, she'd enjoyed it and she'd be more amenable to his apology. But then, once she had a few glasses of wine, she'd be much more understanding. "If I have to haul your pretty little ass up the mountain to meet Sam Morgan, I want to know you can carry some of the load."

"I can haul my own ass, thank you very much. So are you going to take me?"

"I haven't decided yet. But maybe it would be a good idea for you to walk a few miles in Sam Morgan's boots."

"As long as those boots have a fashionable heel and don't make my calves look fat, I'll give it a try."

Sam chuckled softly then took her hand and walked her back to the campsite. As they built a fire, he considered kissing her again…then tugging her sweater over her head…then sliding her skirt up over her hips. He stopped at an idle contemplation of her underwear. Bikini or thong?

"You won't regret this," Sarah said. "Not that you've decided to take me. But if you do, you won't regret it."

Sam smiled. Hell, how could he possibly regret keeping Sarah Cantrell within arm's reach for a few days longer? Though he knew it was mostly about desire, there was something inside him that wanted to show her his view of the world.

Maybe then, she'd understand why he'd lied to protect his privacy. And why he'd always choose the solitude of his life on the mountain over fame and fortune.

2

SARAH POKED at the embers of their campfire with a stick, staring into the glowing coals. They'd finished dinner an hour ago and were sipping another glass of wine after a dessert of Snickers candy bars.

She glanced over her shoulder at Charlie. He sat on the rough log bench, his back braced against the edge of the picnic table, his long legs stretched out in front of him. She turned back to the fire. Why hadn't he tried to kiss her again?

"That was a great meal," he said as she sat down next to him. He picked up the tin cup that held his wine and raised it to her. "My compliments to the chef. I didn't think you'd know your way around a campfire."

"Girl Scout camp, every summer from the age of seven to fifteen. I know how to build a fire and paddle a canoe and sing 'Kumbayah.' Did you expect me to run screaming from the woods at the prospect of cooking over a campfire?"

"I'm not sure what I expected from you," he said, his voice soft and low, his gaze drifting down to her mouth. His arm rested on the table behind her and he began to play with her hair. "I think you might be full of all sorts of surprises."

All this flirting was fun, Sarah mused, and the

kissing was even better. But he still hadn't answered her question. "I need you to take me to Sam Morgan," she said, her tone direct. "I'm willing to do whatever it takes."

A moment later, she realized how her words sounded. Yes, she was willing to live without showers and cell phones, she was willing to trudge up a muddy mountainside with a pack strapped to her back and to cook over a campfire. But if he thought she might be willing to trade sexual favors, then he was sadly mis—

Oh, hell. Who was she trying to fool? Right now, she'd jump at the flimsiest excuse to get naked with Charlie Wilbury. Every time she looked at him, she caught herself imagining what it would be like to discover the body beneath the flannel and denim, to see what a man with all that smoldering sex appeal was like in bed.

"Why is it so important to you?" he asked, his gaze shifting to her mouth.

"It just is. I really want to produce this series. And I usually get what I want."

A long silence grew between them. Maybe she hadn't played this right, Sarah thought. But she didn't want him to string her along. If he wasn't going to take her to Sam, then she'd have to find another way.

"What is it you do back in the big city?" Charlie asked, picking up her hand and toying with her fingers.

"I don't live in a big city. In fact, I live in a small town. Belfort, South Carolina. It's not far from the coast between Charleston and Savannah."

"Answer my question," he said.

"I'm an independent television producer," Sarah explained. "My first project was a—"

"No, no," Charlie interrupted. "I don't want to know about your job. I want to know about you. What do you do? On a typical Saturday night."

"I'd probably be out. Dinner and maybe a movie. Sometimes a concert. A few weekends ago, I went to an art gallery opening." She thought back over the dates she'd had in the last year, noisy parties and crowded theaters. She couldn't remember enjoying a single occasion as much as she'd enjoyed this dinner. Or remember being with a man as attractive as Charlie.

"You must have your pick of men," he said.

"And what do you do on a typical Saturday night?" Sarah said, deftly changing the subject.

"Same thing," he said. "Gallery openings are big in Sutter Gap. Just last week Dub Watley got a new Elvis on velvet and we all stood around at the Lucky Penny and admired it. It's a masterpiece, I tell you."

Sarah laughed. "You're a very charming man, Charlie Wilbury."

"And you're a very beautiful woman, Sarah Cantrell," he replied.

Sarah knew if she just leaned forward slightly he'd kiss her again. It was there, in the soft curl of his smile and the sleepy look in his eyes. She ached to be swept off her feet by a kiss, to be so overwhelmed by a man's touch she lost all sense of time and place. And since she'd met Charlie, she was certain he was the kind of man who could make her wildest fantasies come true.

But bending Charlie to her will had nothing at all to do with sex, she reminded herself. Though she might be tempted to jump into bed with the first sexy wilderness guide to come along the trail, she had to keep her eye on the real prize—Sam Morgan.

"It's getting late," she said. "I should really get back."

He reached out and smoothed a strand of hair from her face. The simple contact had a devastating effect, instantly melting her very last thought of Sam Morgan.

"Sarah, there's something I need to tell you."

Her breath caught and she groaned inwardly. She'd heard those words, that tone of voice, from several men she'd dated. It never signaled good news. "You're married?" she said.

"No!" Charlie replied, as if insulted.

"Then you're getting married. Or you have a steady girlfriend. Or you just got out of a relationship."

He shook his head. "No. No girlfriend."

"Oh," she murmured, her cheeks warming with embarrassment. "Well, that's good to know. So what did you want to tell me?"

Charlie stood, rubbing his palms on his thighs. "It'll wait." He held out his hand to help her to her feet. "I'll just grab our things and we'll be off."

Sarah was grateful he couldn't see her embarrassment in the dark. She watched him by the light of the fire as he packed the remains of their meal into the grocery bag. She'd obviously said or done something that had cooled his desire for her. She hadn't meant to imply that he was a liar or a cheat. It's just that her experiences with men had taught her a few things. But then Charlie wasn't like any other man she'd known.

Maybe his sudden aloofness was for the best. She needed Charlie's help, not his body. And falling into bed with him simply to satisfy a momentary craving would only make things more complicated between them.

As they drove back to Sutter Gap, Sarah thought about the days ahead. If she was forced to spend more time with Charlie, then she'd have to find a way to control her attraction to him. The problem was she had no idea how to make that happen.

THE YELLOW BULB above the motel-room door cast Sarah's face in a soft light. As they stood there, saying their good-nights, Sam was now absolutely certain she was the most exquisite woman he had ever met.

Throughout the evening he'd searched for excuses to touch her, longed for opportunities to kiss her. But then he'd remembered the little lie hanging between them and he'd stopped himself. There'd never seemed to be a perfect moment to tell her.

And now that their "date" was over, all he wanted to do was drag her inside to her bed and make love to her. Yet he knew that would mean crossing a line he didn't want to. He'd always prided himself on being a gentleman. And though he really needed a woman right now, there were limits to how far he'd go to get one.

"I had a wonderful time tonight," Sarah said, her gaze fixed on the front of his jacket.

"So did I," he replied. He reached down and tucked a lock of her auburn hair behind her ear.

Sarah looked up at him and his pulse quickened. This was the moment when need usually overpowered common sense, the moment when a simple kiss would lead to a night in bed.

In the end, Sam didn't have to make the choice—Sarah made it for him. She threw her arms around his neck and kissed him. Not a sweet, gentle first-date kiss, but a hot, frantic take-me-to-bed-sailor kiss. At first, Sam wasn't sure what to do. Though he'd had sex on the brain from the moment he'd set eyes on Sarah, he hadn't expected her to take the lead.

Her body molded to his and with a low groan, Sam furrowed his fingers through her hair and deepened the kiss. His tongue dipped into her mouth, tasting the wine they'd shared earlier. He'd always enjoyed kissing women, but he'd looked at it as a necessary prelude to sex. Kissing Sarah *was* pure sex—it was powerful and stimulating and unsettling. The feel of her mouth on his, her hands skimming over his chest, instantly dissolved any indecision he might have had.

"Invite me in," he whispered.

She fumbled with her purse, refusing to break their kiss, then pressed the key into his hand. Sam reached around to unlock the door and they both stumbled inside. The sound of the door closing was like a starter's pistol and they immediately began to strip off their clothes.

She wanted him as much as he wanted her, that much was clear. Sam had never been so desperate to feel a woman's skin beneath his hands, to revel in the soft curves of her body. When their jackets and sweaters lay on the floor around their feet, he slid his palms up to cup her breasts through her lacy bra.

"Take it off," she whispered against his mouth.

Sam reached around and unhooked her bra. She

let it slip along her arms and drop to the floor. Then he quickly tugged his T-shirt over his head and pulled her back into his embrace. When skin touched skin and her breasts brushed against his chest, desire flooded his senses.

"This doesn't mean I'm going to take you to Sam Morgan," he said, nuzzling her neck.

Sarah furrowed her fingers through his hair and gently tugged his head back. She met his gaze. "And I'm not doing this because I want you to take me to Sam Morgan," she countered. "This is just about the sex, pure and simple."

"Then you expect we're going to have sex?" Sam asked, grinning.

She returned his smile then let her hands drop to the button on his jeans. "We're both adults, we both have needs. I didn't invite you in to play Parcheesi."

"There's nothing standing in our way," he countered. "Nothing except the rest of our clothes."

"Then take them off."

He bent down and untied his boots. She watched as he slid his jeans down and stepped out of them, kicking off his boots and socks along the way. "Better?" Sam asked, standing in just his boxers.

Her gaze drifted along his naked chest and she smiled. "Much better."

"Now you," he urged.

She unzipped her skirt and a moment later, she was standing in just her panties. Sam drew a deep breath and tried to focus his mind. Even in his dream, it hadn't been so intense, so consuming.

He pulled her body against his, drawing her leg up along his hip. She wasn't model thin or surgically enhanced or trainer toned. She was just…real, so soft and beautiful that he ached to touch every part of her.

His shaft strained against the fabric of his boxers, warm against her belly. Slipping his hands beneath her backside, Sam picked her up and wrapped her legs around his waist. He carried her to the bed then knelt down on the mattress, carefully lowering her to the pillows.

Why was he so insane to have her? It wasn't just a physical need with Sarah. He wanted to feel close to her, to connect in a way that was pure and perfect. He barely knew her, yet he was certain that if they shared this moment, he'd find something that had been lost to him long ago.

He'd never really surrendered completely to a woman, not body and soul. He'd always held part of himself back, certain that in doing so, he'd protect himself. He'd been taught early in his life that love could cause as much pain as it did happiness. For once, he wanted to forget his fears and just feel something again—something real.

As he stretched out beside her, she sighed softly and let her hand drift along his torso. Her touch sent a current racing through his body, awakening nerves that had been asleep for months. Slowly, they finished undressing each other, tossing aside what scraps were left between them until they were both naked.

Sam wanted to take her right then, to drag her beneath him and sink into her until he lost himself in her heat and damp. But suddenly a brief night of pleasure didn't seem so appealing. He wanted to know that this wouldn't be the only time he would make love to this special woman, that she would find her way into his bed again and again.

He stared down into her eyes, caressing her face with his fingertips. There was still a lie standing between them. But he didn't care. It didn't matter what had brought them together, all that mattered was this magic now between them. "All right," he murmured, dropping a kiss on her lips. "I'll take you to Sam Morgan."

Sarah smiled, then crawled on top of him, weaving her fingers through his and pinning his arms above his head. "I'm glad we got that out of the way." She kissed him lightly, then crawled off the bed.

With a soft groan, Sam sat up. "Where are you going?"

She picked up his jeans from the floor and withdrew his wallet, then held it out, just beyond his reach. Sam felt a sliver of fear shoot through him. All she had to do was open it and she'd find out that the man in her bed wasn't really Charlie Wilbury. And that would probably be the end of their evening together. Maybe he ought to tell her the truth right now, before it blew up in his face.

He held his breath as she opened the wallet then smiled. "You must have been a Boy Scout," she said.

"Why is that?" Sam asked warily.

She held up a strip of three condoms then tossed the wallet back on the floor. "Always prepared." As she slowly crossed back to the bed, she opened one of the foil packages. "Were you thinking you might get lucky tonight?"

He'd hoped for luck. But this wasn't just luck, having a woman like Sarah, holding her in his arms. This was something much more profound. He felt as if he were standing at a crossroads along the long trail that was his life. He could continue down the path he was on, taking pleasure when it was offered and then walking away without a second thought.

Or he could turn in a different direction, wander down another trail, and allow himself to feel all the emotions that went along with desire and need and passion. For the first time in his life, he wanted more. All this, inspired by the incredible woman before him. But was he really ready to accept the risks?

Sam braced himself for her touch, trying to maintain control as she sheathed him. "It isn't luck," he murmured. "I knew we'd end up here. It was fate." He grabbed her hand to keep her from sending him over the edge right then and there. "Maybe we should take this a little slower," he suggested, his gaze skimming over her naked body.

"I've waited too long already," she said as she crawled back on top of him.

"So have I." Days, months, years. For whatever reason, he somehow felt it had all led to this point in his life. But now, it was time to let the past go and surrender to the present.

Sam trailed a finger from her shoulder to her breast, teasing at her nipple. When she closed her eyes, a thrill raced through him. He wanted to learn what made her moan, wanted to memorize every reaction so that he knew her body like no other man had. He grabbed her hips and brought her closer. Her expression gradually shifted from anticipation to sheer bliss as she settled herself above him, the tip of his shaft slipping inside her a tiny bit at a time.

Though they'd begun unhurriedly, passion soon overcame restraint. She moved above him, her eyes closed, her head tipped back. He watched her, sensing the subtleties in her expression as her pleasure mounted. Waves of desire washed over him, and he tried to focus, but the urge to come made it impossible to think rationally anymore.

Though it had been months since he'd had sex, somehow it felt as if he'd never been with a woman before. Every sensation with Sarah was new, extreme, electric, her body a perfect match for his. Sam reached up and drew her toward him, his lips searching for hers, craving the taste of her mouth.

It felt so right, his body one with hers, and everything else between them stripped away. He didn't want to come yet, but there was nothing he could do to slow her pace. So he reached between them and began to stroke her at the spot where they were joined, teasing her sensitive nub with his fingers, urging her toward her own release.

Sarah sighed softly and began to move faster and he knew she was close. And then she froze, her eyes opening and her breath catching in her throat, her fingernails digging into his shoulders. Their gazes met and in that instant, he felt the connection, an absolute surrender between them.

A moan slipped from her lips and then she tumbled over the edge, convulsing around him, sinking down until he was buried deep inside of her. A moment later, Sam joined her, giving over to the shudders that wracked his body, driving into her one last time.

When the last of their passion had been spent, he gently drew her down beside him, pulling the bedcovers over them both. He closed his eyes as he languidly toyed with her hair, his lips pressed against her forehead.

For so long, he'd been all alone in the world, with no one to trust but himself. First his mother, then his father, and then his best friend, they'd all left him, taking tiny bits of his heart along with them until there was barely enough left to pump blood through his body.

Sam pressed his hand to his chest and felt the beat, sure and strong. He was still alive and he could still feel something. And though he wasn't sure what it was, he did know that Sarah Cantrell had made it happen.

She curled into his body, her breathing soft and even. Once upon a time, one night of passion might have been enough, but it wasn't anymore. Not nearly. He had the distinct impression that no matter how many nights he spent in bed with Sarah, no matter how many times they made love, it might never be enough.

SARAH STARED at herself in the bathroom mirror, noticing the dark smudges beneath her eyes. She hadn't slept more than three or four hours, and most of that had come just after sunrise, after Charlie had left. He'd kissed her goodbye and promised to return at ten to take her shopping for new hiking boots and a proper backpack.

She couldn't help but wonder if last night had been a mistake. A simple one-night stand could turn very complicated if either person wanted more than just one night. And after last night, she did want more.

It might have been much easier if Charlie Wilbury had been a disaster in the bedroom. But he seemed to sense her every need, to read her desire and satisfy it in the most wonderful way. She'd been entirely unprepared for it to be so... "Phenomenal," Sarah murmured. Even now, the thought of what they'd shared sent a shiver coursing through her body.

But this trip wasn't supposed to be about getting laid. Her professional future now rested with a man who'd seen her naked and who probably wanted to see her naked again—a man who'd touched her body in the most intimate ways and who'd brought her to three of the most earth-shattering orgasms she'd ever experienced. Yes, Charlie Wilbury knew exactly how to take her right over the edge of reason and that made him a very dangerous man.

The temptation to experience it all over again would be unbearable. But they'd both gone into this expecting a single night of mutual satisfaction. She couldn't change the rules now. Which meant she'd have to suck it up. Because she was going to have to spend at least the next few days with Charlie if she wanted to get to Sam Morgan. Sarah closed her eyes and sighed. "Just don't forget why you came here," she murmured.

All this passion was very distracting. When it came down to it, she had a life and a job back in Charleston. And Charlie was just an attractive man who lived in Sutter Gap. As long as she reminded herself it had just been great sex, then maybe she'd be able to maintain her perspective.

"He's just a man," she muttered. As far as she was concerned, there wasn't any man on the planet who could be completely trusted. Her father had been shining proof of that theory.

Sarah had adored him as any daughter should. From her very first memories of him, she'd been certain he'd hung the moon and the stars. And then one day, when she was ten years old, she'd heard her parents arguing about another woman.

Gradually, she'd come to understand why her mother had called him a philanderer. And she'd also learned her father's infidelities were common knowledge around Belfort. That's when Bill Cantrell had fallen from hero status to nothing more than a humiliating embarrassment to his family.

As the eldest of three daughters, Sarah had taken on the responsibility of maintaining the facade of normalcy. And as her mother had shattered into pieces, Sarah had become her only confidante, forced to listen to the sordid details of her father's ongoing affair with his secretary and obliged to give her mother marital advice.

It might not have been so bad had her mother chosen to divorce her father. But instead, Susan Cantrell had ignored her husband's behavior, sinking into a deep melancholy that never seemed to lift. She couldn't bear to lose the man she loved, so she'd settled for what she could get—another woman's leftovers.

Was it any wonder Sarah didn't trust men? She turned on the cold water and splashed her face, hoping it might clear her head. When she looked back at her image in the mirror, droplets of water still clung to her lashes. She licked her damp lips, still tender from the night before. "Get a grip. He's just a man," she repeated. "Nothing more."

A knock sounded on the door and Sarah glanced over her shoulder. It was barely nine and he'd said ten. She still hadn't decided what she was going to say to him. Of course, she could trot out the old "we're both adults" line and take it from there. Or she could just tell him the sex was great, but it had been a mistake to mix business with pleasure. Or she could simply drag him back to bed and see what else transpired.

As she walked to the door, her mind filled with thoughts of spending the day in bed with Charlie. But it wasn't just about his prowess between the sheets. She wanted to be with him, to talk to him and to touch him, to learn about the kind of man he was. This wasn't a fish she was anxious to throw back.

After grabbing a towel, she quickly dried her face as she walked to the door. She'd go with the "we're both adults" speech and if he insisted on dragging her back to bed, she wouldn't protest. After all, what harm could just a few more hours with a naked and aroused man possibly do?

But when she opened the motel room door, she found Hattie Wilbury standing outside. Hattie owned the Gap View Motor Lodge and had made Sarah's introductions into Sutter Gap society—including an introduction to her cousin Carter Wilbury, Sam Morgan's good friend.

"Mornin'," Hattie said. "Would you like me to make up the room?"

Sarah shook her head. "Maybe later. I'm going into Asheville this morning. And then I'm probably going to be gone for a few days, but I want to keep some of my things here, so I'll pay for the room for another week."

"Where are you going?" Hattie asked.

"To see Sam Morgan. Charlie Wilbury is taking me."

Hattie's eyebrow sprang up. "Is that so? Charlie Wilbury?"

Sarah nodded. "I understand he's related to you. Is he your nephew or your cousin or—"

"Charlie is kind of the black sheep of the family." Hattie paused. "You say he's takin' you to Asheville this morning? Now that's funny, 'cause I saw Charlie headin' out of town an hour ago and he looked like he wasn't comin' back."

Sarah gasped. "What?"

"Mmm-hmm. He and Carter were walking toward the old logging road and Charlie was carrying his pack. Looks like they're headed up to see Sam Morgan."

"But—but we had a deal. I'm paying him to take *me* to Sam Morgan!"

"He's got your money?" Hattie asked.

"No, not yet. But he agreed last night while we were—" She swallowed hard. "Well, he agreed."

"I guess he changed his mind, then," Hattie said. "No surprise there. That boy has a way of dancing around the truth if you ask me. You're better rid of him. He's trouble."

"I'm beginning to realize that," Sarah muttered, fuming. She turned and hurried back into the room, gathering up her clothes and stuffing them into her suitcase. "I'm going up that damn mountain with or without his help. If I move fast enough maybe I can catch him."

"That would be a might unlikely," Hattie said. "Unless, of course, you get someone to drive you up Dewey Road. The trail crosses the road about two miles in. You'd beat them there by about an hour."

Sarah grabbed her purse and yanked out her wallet, then held out all the cash she had. "I'll pay you to show me the way."

Hattie frowned. "No need to pay me. I can take you up there and then I'll bring your car back." She paused, as if weighing her next words. "Are you sure you want to do this? If Sam Morgan doesn't want to talk to you, hiking up that mountain isn't going to change his mind."

"I've been waiting in Sutter Gap for ten days now. If he won't come to me, I'm going to him. And Mr. Wilbury is going to take me, whether he wants to or not."

"How are you going to convince him to do something he doesn't want to do?"

Sarah snatched up her sneakers and tugged them onto her feet. "I can be very persuasive," she muttered. With that, she zipped up her suitcase and hefted it off the bed. "I'm ready. Let's go."

They walked out to her car and put the suitcase in the trunk. When she slipped behind the wheel, she threw the car into gear and headed out to the road. She was not about to let Charlie Wilbury get the better of her.

They'd driven about a mile when she glanced over at Hattie. "So, what do you know about him?"

"Sam Morgan is a rascal."

"I was talking about Charlie Wilbury."

"Oh, he's a rascal, too. Can't trust a thing he says. And if I were you, I'd keep tight hold of my panties when I was around him."

Sarah gasped, a flush warming her cheeks. "Then he's a…"

"Casanova," Hattie finished. "Slick as a button. Loves 'em and leaves 'em. Just watch yourself. I wouldn't want him breakin' your heart."

Sarah watched the road ahead, slowing for a wide

curve. Maybe she should have learned a little more about Charlie before she'd actually slept with the man, she mused. But how would she have found out? Everyone in Sutter Gap was so tight-lipped—everyone except Hattie—it made casual conversation impossible. "I will watch myself. And thank you for the advice."

Maybe if she'd had a little more self-control, she wouldn't have found herself in this mess. From the first moment she'd met him, she'd caught herself having lascivious thoughts about him, about the body beneath the flannel and denim. He was everything a real man was supposed to be.

Yes, and he was everything a man wasn't supposed to be—deceitful, conniving, untrustworthy. He'd made promises he'd never intended to keep. And to make matters worse, he'd made those promises in bed!

"It's right up here," Hattie said.

After shaking her head clear, Sarah squinted against the sun and pulled the car over to the side of the road. A wide path had been cut through the woods, but it was overgrown with vegetation.

"If you wait here, I expect he'll be coming along shortly," Hattie said. "He'll come out of the woods right there."

"Maybe you should wait with me," Sarah suggested.

"I need to get back to the motel. But I can come back up here 'round noon," Hattie offered. "If you're still here, I'll take you back. Don't worry, there aren't any man-eatin' wolves or bears in these parts. And there'll be a few cars comin' by if you need help before then. Just wave one down."

Sarah nodded, then popped the trunk and got out of the car. She dragged her suitcase to the side of the road, then waved to Hattie as the woman made a U-turn and headed back toward town.

With a soft curse, she sat down on the edge of her bag and contemplated what she'd say to Charlie when she saw him again. First, she'd tell him exactly what she thought of his business practices. And then, she'd warn him that if he ever touched her again, he could say goodbye to the family jewels. And for good measure, she'd insult his prowess in bed. A man with such an inflated ego deserved to be taken down a peg or two.

The muffled sound of a cell phone broke the silence, startling Sarah. She jumped up and pushed her suitcase flat, then unzipped it. The phone hadn't worked since she'd arrived in Sutter Gap. She found it buried beneath her underwear and flipped it open. "Hello?"

"Where were you last night?" Libby demanded. "I called your room four times and then I fell asleep. And when I called the motel a few minutes ago, the lady said you'd left. I figured maybe you were on your way home. That's why I tried your cell phone."

Sarah sat down in the open suitcase, glad to hear a friendly voice. "I was out last night. On a date. Or maybe it wasn't a date. I'm not sure anymore."

"I thought you said all the men were—"

"I was wrong. I found one that wasn't so bad. In fact, he was really good." She sighed. "Really, really good, if you get my drift."

Libby moaned. "You slept with a man?"

"No, I slept with a goat."

"You know what I mean," Libby said.

"Yes, and we didn't do much sleeping. But he was hot, so I have an excuse. And if I'm going to have a one-night stand, I might as well have it here where no one knows me, right?"

"Are you trying to convince me or convince yourself?" Libby asked.

"As long as he was willing, I wasn't going to say no. Men like him don't come along every day. I just got swept away. But believe me, it won't happen again."

"There won't be any…"

"Repeat performances? No. I caught him and now I'm throwing him back. I thought he was different, but he's just like all the other men I've known. He's a liar and a jerk."

"Sleeping with a man isn't always as simple as it seems, Sarah. Sometimes it can make a complete mess of everything."

"What about you and Trey? Look how things turned out for you. Don't forget, I was the one who urged you to seduce him and I haven't heard any complaints on that score. So sometimes it does work out, right?"

"I carried a torch for Trey for years. And I consider myself lucky that it turned out as well as it did. It just as easily could have been a disaster."

"Well, don't worry, there will be no torch carrying here. This was just about lust and nothing else. And now that I've scratched that itch, I can get back to business again."

"Maybe you should come home and think about producing a nice little gardening show. Leave Sam Morgan to his nuts and berries."

"I'm going up that mountain with Charlie Wilbury."

"Who's Charlie Wilbury?"

"The man who's taking me up the mountain," Sarah said, then added morosely, "And the man I slept with last—"

A rustling in the bushes caught Sarah's attention and with a shriek, she scrambled to her feet and ran out into the center of the road. Whatever animal was hiding in the shadows, she didn't want it coming near her.

"What is it?" Libby asked.

"Nothing. I just— Listen, I have to go. I don't want to use up the battery on my phone now that it actually works. I'll try to call you tomorrow."

Libby said goodbye and Sarah flipped off the power on her phone. Then she hurried back to her suitcase and rummaged through it for a weapon. Grabbing her hairdryer, she tested its weight. If she swung it from the cord, she might be able to knock an animal out, giving her time to climb the nearest tree.

A long string of curses slipped from her lips as she pulled her suitcase out into the middle of road. If finding Sam Morgan hadn't been her number-one priority, she would have just dragged her suitcase back down the highway and gone home, putting as much distance as she could between her raging hormones and Charlie Wilbury's seductive smile.

But she had a job to do and she intended to get it done, with or without Charlie's help.

3

THE CANOPY of bare branches overhead cast shadows on the trail and the chilly spring breeze caught dry leaves, sending them swirling in the air. Sam stopped and grabbed his water bottle, then offered it to Carter.

"Are you sure you ought to be going back so soon?" Carter asked. "Weatherman predicts rain and cold for tonight. You could have picked a better day to leave."

"I'll be fine," Sam said. "If I keep up this pace, I can get to the cabin before sundown. I want to start resupplying as soon as possible. I've been thinking about digging a well up there and that will probably take most of the summer."

"What's the real reason you're heading back up?" Carter asked.

"Same reason as always. Civilization is a little too crowded for me."

Carter eyed him warily. "You sure it's not that pretty little thing you spent the night with?" He held out his hands. "Hey, you left your truck parked in front of the motel. Everyone in Sutter Gap knows what was going on in there, so there's no use denying it."

Sam shrugged. "Maybe I'm not interested in what

she has to offer." He took the bottle from Carter, tucked it into the side pocket of his pack then continued up the trail.

Last night had been the first time he'd allowed himself to feel something for a woman, beyond indifference. When he was making love to Sarah, he'd felt a spark inside him, a tiny electric shock that made every sensation, more intense, more real.

For the first time in a long time, he felt like he was moving forward. Though Sam wasn't sure where he was going yet, at least he wasn't standing still, as he had been for far too long. There was something out there, just beyond his reach, and it was as if Sarah had been sent to show him the way.

Was it happiness? Contentment? Until now, those things had eluded him. But it hadn't always been that way. There had been a time when he'd been happy. As an only child, his parents had doted on him, loved him more than most parents ever could. He'd lived in a small town in Connecticut, in a big house with a yard. He'd had friends to play with and a dog that slept with him every night. And then, in the course of just a month, everything had changed.

He'd been twelve when his mother had gone into the hospital. Twenty-seven days later, he'd stood beside her grave, his happy life suddenly not so happy anymore. He'd tried not to cry, the emotions causing an ache so strong that it had stolen his breath away. But to shed a single tear would have been weak and self-indulgent. He'd needed to be strong for his father.

In the end, Sam's mask of stoic acceptance hadn't helped. Over the next five years, his father had grad-

ually drunk himself to death and when Sam had
stood beside his grave, it had almost been with a
sense of relief that his father's pain had finally ended.

Sam had seen how powerful love could be, how
it could take a strong, successful, vibrant man and re-
duce him to nothing more than an empty shell. He'd
promised himself that he'd never be that vulnerable.
And he hadn't, keeping everyone he met at arm's
length.

But then, he found a friend in Jeff Warren and Jeff
had invited him into his big, noisy family. And for a
short time, Sam had allowed himself to be happy
again. And in a heartbeat, it had been snatched away.

Was that what would happen with Sarah? Last
night, he'd allowed himself a tiny bit of happiness.
Sam wasn't sure why Sarah had been the one to
break through the protective wall he'd built around
his heart, but she was. He'd experienced something
pure and good with her. Only later had he remembered it was tainted with a lie.

She'd made love to Charlie Wilbury, not Sam Morgan. And if she'd known the truth, she might not
have tumbled into bed so willingly. And now, he was
doing what he did best—retreating, finding a place
where he wouldn't have to deal with his emotions.

The thrills he'd shared with Sarah weren't much
different than the thrill he got climbing a mountain
or jumping out of a plane. His mind now fixed on
that one moment when his body had become part of
hers and she'd taken him over the edge, the rush of
adrenaline and the waves of exhilaration. He'd acted
on impulse again, ignoring the dangers just so he
could feel something—anything. Had it been worth
the risk?

"What do you plan to do about Sarah Cantrell?" Carter asked.

"Nothing," Sam said. "Sooner or later, she'll give up and go home."

"She's powerful stubborn, that one," Carter said.

"I can wait a lot longer than she can. And no one knows where to find me except you. As long as you don't show her the way, I'm safe. And you're not going to show her, right?"

Carter nodded and they continued hiking. Up ahead, the trail widened and Sam knew they were coming up on Dewey Road, the point where Carter would turn back to town and he would go on alone. But as they approached the clearing, they slowed their pace. A solitary figure sat in the middle of the road, perched on a huge black suitcase.

"Like I said," Carter murmured, "that gal is powerful stubborn."

Sam glanced back down the trail, ready to turn around and go in the opposite direction. Then he looked back at Sarah and watched as she slowly stood. There'd be no going back now. "Aw, hell."

"I'm gonna turn around and head home, now," Carter said. "Y'all have a safe trip."

Carter quickly disappeared into the woods behind him, as Sam slowly approached Sarah. He studied her expression, wondering just how mad she was. Though he knew walking out on her hadn't been the best way to handle the situation, he honestly couldn't think of a better alternative.

"We had a deal," she shouted, her eyes sparkling with anger, her fists hitched on her hips.

The next instant she hurled something at him. He side-stepped it and it crashed behind him on the road. Sam turned to find a hairdryer in pieces on the pavement. "What the hell are you doing?"

"What are *you* doing? You told me you were going to take me to Sam Morgan. You promised!"

"I changed my mind," Sam said. God, she was beautiful. Enraged, asleep, aroused, it made no difference. He could spend days just studying the way her emotions played across her features. And now that she was standing here in front of him, Sam had to wonder at the sheer idiocy that had possessed him that morning. He should be in bed with her right now, enjoying the very pleasures they'd experienced the night before, not beating himself up over a stupid lie he'd told.

"You can't change your mind," she said. "I won't let you. I'm coming with you."

Once she found out who she'd really slept with, she'd head right back to Sutter Gap. "Listen, I don't think Sam Morgan will be interested in your deal. In fact, I know he won't. So this is all just a big waste of time. Go back to town, get in your car and forget about him." And forget about me, he added silently.

"You can't speak for him," she said.

"I'm pretty sure I can," Sam said. "In fact, I'm—"

"Well, I won't accept that. If you don't agree to take me, then I'll just follow you around the woods until you do."

"Right. And that'll last about an hour." He adjusted the waist strap on his backpack and walked toward the other side of the road. There was no talking to her and absolutely no way to explain his deception. He'd be smarter to keep his mouth shut and walk away. "Good luck and it was nice knowing you." He didn't glance back and for a moment,

Sam thought she'd given up. But when she shouted at him again, he knew he was doomed.

"Is this about last night?" she demanded. "Because it shouldn't be. We were two consenting adults and I think we both got what we wanted. But don't get any funny ideas about us and why I'm here. If you think I'm going to sleep with you again just because I need your help, then you're sadly mistaken. I will not trade sex for Sam Morgan. We made a business deal and I will be paying you for your services from now on."

Sam chuckled as he slowly turned. "My services? And was last night covered or can I expect an extra big tip for that?"

Sarah pulled out the handle on her suitcase and rolled it across the road to where he stood. "I'm not going to give up," she said. "So you can quit acting like such an ass and take me up that mountain."

Sam ground his teeth. Hell, he'd tried to walk away, given it his best shot. But maybe a few more days with Sarah Cantrell was all he needed to prove to himself that women like her, that any woman, had no place in his life. "Suit yourself."

"I can take care of myself, just lead the way."

Sam gave her one last look before he started back into the woods. He could hear her stumbling around in the brush as she tried to drag her suitcase through impossibly tangled scrub. A tiny smile tugged at his lips. This wouldn't even last an hour. He'd give her fifteen minutes before she was ready to give up. Then she'd toddle off down the mountain and be out of his life for good.

Every instinct told him to send her packing, to forget about what he'd felt when they'd touched each other. Yet with every step she took, Sam silently urged her on, wanting just a few more hours, or maybe a day or two, with this woman.

He couldn't seem to let her go, so maybe she'd have to be the one to walk away.

SARAH YANKED her suitcase over a fallen log, cursing with every step she took. She was cold, she was tired and she'd only been hiking for a couple of hours. This mountain man stuff was hard work. But she was determined to keep up with Charlie.

She stopped to catch her breath, watching him walk about thirty feet in front of her. For a thousand dollars, he should at least give her a hand with her luggage. After all, it was his fault she didn't have the proper equipment. She had a good mind to report him to whatever professional association oversaw the behavior of mountain guides.

Frustrated, Sarah sat down on the edge of her suitcase and crossed her ankle over her knee. Her sneakers were soaked and muddy and her wet socks had worn raw spots on her heels. And if she didn't know better, she'd swear her toes were frostbitten.

Wincing, she untied her shoe and tugged it off, then massaged her numb toes. She stood on one foot and rummaged through her bag for a pair of dry socks. As always, she'd overpacked, the pretty clothes now nothing more than dead weight to haul around the forest.

"Leave it."

The sound of his voice startled her and she pitched forward. At the last second, Charlie grabbed her waist and pulled her up to stand in front of him. The feel of his hands beneath her jacket stole her breath away. Her knees wobbled and her mind flashed back to the previous night, to the sensation of his hands on her naked body.

"I—I can't just leave all my stuff here."

"Pick out what you need and dump the rest. You can stop for it on your way down. Just make sure there's no food inside or the animals will drag it off."

"What animals?" Sarah asked, envisioning hungry mountain lions running through the forest with her Samsonite in their fangs.

"Black bears. Or maybe a tenacious squirrel. They'll chew right though the suitcase if they smell something good inside."

Charlie let go of her then shrugged out of his backpack, leaning it against a nearby tree. Her gaze fixed on his mouth. What that man could do with his mouth, she mused, a tiny shiver skittering up her spine. She contemplated throwing herself into his arms right then and there. But she wasn't entirely sure he'd welcome her advances.

"I've got room in my pack for a few more things," he said. "We'll be able to move a lot faster if you don't carry anything at all."

He picked through her suitcase and pulled out a fresh pair of socks. Sarah leaned back against a tree as he gently rubbed her aching toes. Then, to her horror, he took her foot and slid it under his flannel shirt, pressing it up against his warm belly.

Sarah bit back a moan and tried to ignore the wonderful sensations his fingers aroused. He massaged her foot and when the blood was again circulating, he slipped on the sock and helped her back into her damp shoe. Her heart slammed in her chest as he carefully tended to her opposite foot, his thumbs working at the cramped arch.

"Is that better?" he asked.

She nodded then swallowed hard. "You know, maybe now might be a good time for you to explain why you have a giant bug up your butt. If you'd like to discuss what happened last night, I'm perfectly willing. We can dissect the entire evening, moment by moment, if that's what you want."

Charlie chuckled softly. "That won't be necessary."

"But I think we need to get a few things—"

"Straight?" He shook his head. "Last night was… last night. Nothing more, nothing less. No strings here, I promise."

Sarah straightened. "Exactly my thoughts," she said. Though she wouldn't have chosen "nothing" as an accurate description for their night together. Last night had really been *something*. Not just great, but fabulous, unforgettable, earth-shattering. So why wasn't *he* thinking about throwing her into the bushes and seducing her all over again?

Maybe she hadn't been as fabulous as she'd thought. Sarah rewound the night in her head, remembering his reactions when she'd touched him, recalling the words he'd whispered in her ear as he'd moved inside her. If he hadn't enjoyed himself, then he really ought to explore a career in porn films.

Charlie slowly stood, rubbing his hands on his thighs. "So, what's it going to be?"

She frowned. "Well, I suppose if it happens again I wouldn't be opposed to the idea, but—"

"I meant the suitcase," he said. "What do you want to take along?"

She felt a flush of embarrassment creep up her cheeks and bent down to search through her belongings. A thick wool sweater was the only thing she knew she'd need. The rest was just—the assortment of clothes blurred before her eyes.

Before she took one more step down the trail, she needed to know where she stood. All this uncertainty was driving her crazy. Sarah spun to face him and threw her arms around his neck.

She saw that Charlie was watching her warily. When she pushed up on her toes and leaned into him, Sarah felt his body tense. And when she ran her tongue along his lower lip, a soft groan rumbled in his chest. Teasing at the crease of his mouth, she dared him to respond. And when he bent closer to kiss her, Sarah smiled and drew back, satisfied she had her answer. "I thought so," she murmured.

She wanted to leave it there, safe in the knowledge that his desire for her hadn't abated. But Charlie had other ideas. His hands quickly moved to her face and he slid his fingers through her tangled hair, pulling her closer. She held her breath, waiting, wondering how far he'd take it. An instant later, his mouth was on hers, his lips warm and damp.

His kiss was a carefully planned assault, meant to destroy every ounce of her self-control. His tongue flicked at hers in a tantalizing caress, reminding her of what they'd shared the night before.

It didn't matter that he'd broken his promise to her, or that he'd put her through torture in the past few hours, or even that he saw her as nothing more than just a good time in bed. She still wanted him, craved the feel of his hands on her body and the heady taste of his tongue in her mouth.

He stepped back and when her eyes fluttered open, Sarah found him staring down at her, a smile curling the corners of his mouth. Her little test had been turned against her and now he knew that he was the one in complete control.

Reaching up, he dragged his thumb along her lower lip. "If you're coming with me," he murmured, "then you have to do exactly what I tell you. Agreed?"

She nodded. After that kiss, she felt like putty in his hands. Sarah tried to speak, to think of a witty comeback, but her brain had lost its ability to form a coherent thought.

"Decide what you want to take and we'll put it in my pack."

Obediently, Sarah turned around, waiting for her pulse to slow and her breathing to return to normal. This was progress. At least now, he'd agreed to help her. She removed her laptop from the suitcase and handed it to him.

"Are you really going to need this?" he asked, arching his brow.

"My proposal is on there. The budgets, the production schedule. I can't leave it behind. I need it for my presentation."

"It's got to weigh six or seven pounds," he said.

"Then I'll carry it," she said. She found her Black-Berry and her cell phone and tucked them into her jacket pocket. Then she pulled out her cosmetics bag and handed it to him.

"You don't need this," he said, peering at the contents through the clear vinyl.

"You haven't seen me in the morning," she replied.

"Yes, I have." His voice was so low it sent a tremor racing through her. "And you don't need makeup. You need warm clothes and dry socks. That's what it all comes down to out here, Sarah. The basics of survival. Water, warmth, food, shelter. A few tools, a way to start a fire. When you strip it all down, life is really pretty simple."

She reached into her bag and pulled out a wad of underwear, lacy bras and panties. It may be simple, but a girl still needed clean underwear. She shoved the wad of silk and lace at him and he plucked at a black bra.

"I guess I can find room for these," he said with a sexy grin.

"I get the feeling you find this all very amusing."

"Just think, by the time you get up the mountain, you might just understand why Sam Morgan lives the way he does."

Maybe, Sarah mused. But that wasn't really the big question in her mind. What she couldn't wait to find out was if Charlie Wilbury considered sex one of the "basics of survival."

THEY STOPPED to set up camp a few hours before the sun went down. Sam had wanted to push on, but he could tell Sarah's patience was seriously frayed and her energy flagging. Her shoes were caked with mud and her face scratched by the branches they'd had to push through, but she hadn't complained. She was stubborn to a fault and Sam admired her for that.

In truth, there were a lot of things he admired about Sarah. Yes, she had a perfect body and a lush mouth and striking green eyes. And she knew exactly how to please a man in bed. But it was her sense of humor and the slightly off-center way she had of looking at life that he found so attractive. And she didn't play the coy, manipulative games that some women found so entertaining. If she didn't like something, she said so, without mincing words.

Hell, if he had wanted his life turned into a television show, then Sarah would probably be the one he'd want to do it. It might even be fun, working with her and seeing her every day. But he had no illusions that they'd have a future together. Sam Morgan had no intention of falling in love.

"How much farther do we have to go?" she asked, slipping out of her shoes and sliding her feet closer to the fire.

"A ways," Sam said as he searched for a spot to set up the small tent. He grabbed the poles from the tent bag and assembled them. "About a mile up the trail, we're going to start to climb and then it will be about four more hours. As the crow flies, it's really not that far, but the trail is so rough it takes time."

She glanced around, rubbing her arms against the chill. "What do you suppose he's hiding from out here?" she asked.

Sam fumbled with the tent poles and they clattered in the silence of the woods. "Why would you think he's hiding?"

She shrugged. "I don't know. A man comes out here, leaving society behind. There must be something he's trying to escape. Something he afraid of in the real world."

"Maybe he's just looking for solitude," Sam said. "Absolute, utter solitude. Can you blame him? The world's a pretty noisy place."

"But that's not an answer. Sooner or later, you

have to have some human contact, make some kind of connection. We're not meant to spend our lives all alone."

Sam thought about her words as he finished setting up the tent. She'd made a point. Normal people didn't live like hermits in the middle of the wilderness. But then, maybe he wasn't normal. Maybe the things that made other people happy just didn't work for him.

Until he'd met Sarah, he'd never questioned his decision to live in the wilderness. But since she'd walked into his life, he'd been forced to wonder just what kept him here, all alone, so far from other humans. Maybe this wasn't just about Jeff anymore. Maybe it went a lot deeper. What was he afraid of?

Sam walked over to his pack and unhooked his sleeping bag, then tossed it inside the tent. "I'm going to make some supper. If you want to rest inside, I'll call you when it's ready."

Sarah shook her head. "No, I'm all right here." She tucked her feet up under her. "Thank you for agreeing to take me along, Charlie. I may not have said it, but I am grateful."

"Why is this so important to you?" Sam asked as he tended the fire.

"It just is." She tipped her head back and sighed. "It's silly, really. Or maybe it's pathetic, depending upon how you look at it."

"Tell me," Sam urged.

"My best friend got married last fall and now she's having a baby and her life is coming together in this storybook way. And suddenly, I feel like there's a big void in my life, like I've somehow missed out on something. Most women my age have a husband and a family. But I don't want a husband and a family, so I need to make a success of my career."

"And Sam Morgan will make you feel like a success?" he asked.

"I don't know," she replied. "I told you it sounded silly and now that I've actually said it, it sounds perfectly ridiculous. I'm just afraid if I don't make a good life for myself, then I'll never have a good life. I'm not going to wait for a man to make it happen, that's for damn sure."

"There was a time when I was obsessed with my work," Sam commented.

"Obsessed with wandering around in the forest?" she asked.

"That's not what I've always done. I used to have a real job and I used to make real money. Most people considered me a success. And then one day, I just walked away. Left it all behind."

Sarah studied him for a long moment, curiosity suffusing her expression. "Why?"

"Because I didn't enjoy it anymore. The way I see it, sometimes you have to know when to cut your losses and move on. The things you think will make you happy sometimes just trap you in a life you never wanted in the first place."

"Are you happy now?" Sarah asked.

Sam slowly stood. Now there was a question. He'd never really thought about it. "Right now? At this very instant?"

She nodded.

"Yeah," Sam said, absolutely certain of his answer. "I'm happy." And as he said the words, he realized that they were true. Right now, standing here in the woods with Sarah staring up at him, the light from the fire illuminating her lovely face, he felt good. In truth, he was more content than he'd been in a very, very long time.

"Do you think Sam Morgan is a lost cause for me?"

Sam smiled and shook his head. "No one is a lost cause," he murmured. "For all I know, once you pitch your idea, he might jump at the chance."

He grabbed a tin cup from his mess kit and crossed to the fire. The water in the small coffeepot had come to a boil and he added a bit of instant coffee to the cup, then filled it. Carefully, he handed it to Sarah. "Here, this will warm you up."

Her fingers brushed against his as she took the cup and a flood of heat raced up his arm. Strange how such simple contact could throw him completely off balance. He was starting to get used to the feeling, this crazy combination of desire and apprehension.

"Thanks," she said. She set the cup near the fire, then stood and glanced around. "What exactly is the bathroom situation here? Is there some kind of back-woods etiquette to it or do I just…wander off?"

"You just go," he said, nodding in the direction of a thicket of bushes.

Sarah winced. "That's what I thought." She reached into her jacket pocket and pulled out a crumpled tissue. "If I'm not back in a few minutes, don't come looking for me."

Sam watched as she disappeared into the trees. He continued with dinner preparations, mixing a packet of ramen noodles into a pot of boiling water. He was just setting the pan near the fire when a scream split the silence.

He'd taken no more than a step in the direction of the cry when Sarah came hurtling out of the trees, her eyes wide, her hair disheveled and her jeans unzipped. When she saw him she stopped short, gasping for breath.

"What is it?"

"Nothing," she murmured, her hands trembling. "Are—are there any poisonous snakes out there?"

"Why?"

"I think I've been bitten."

"Where?"

"On my—my right cheek."

Sam knew full well that any snake living in the immediate vicinity was probably in deep hibernation from the cold. But as a responsible wilderness guide, it was his duty to address the client's concerns. "Let me see," he said. He strode over to her and hooked his thumb under her chin, examining her face for any wounds.

"Not that cheek," Sarah said. "The other cheek."

Sam chuckled. "All right. Let's give it a look."

"No! Giving you a close-up view of my butt would be the ultimate humiliation. I think I'd prefer to die from the poison."

"Come on, Sarah. Just let me check it out to be sure."

Reluctantly, she turned her back to him and tugged her jeans down slightly. Craning her neck to see over her shoulder, she watched as he ran his hand over the gentle curve of her hip. He couldn't see a single mark on her perfect skin, but found himself caught by the two tiny dimples at the base of her spine.

"I don't know," Sam murmured, his hand resting on her hip. "I suppose it could be a snakebite. Maybe I should suck out the venom."

"Don't you dare!" Sarah cried. "If anyone is going to suck on my butt, it will be a medical professional."

"All right. But that venom can work very quickly. You could be dead by the time we get you to the hospital."

Sarah sighed, shaking her head. "All right. Go ahead."

Sam stifled a laugh. God, it was fun to mess with her. Especially when he could enjoy a nice view of her backside at the same time. He spanned her waist with his hands. "Hold still," he said. He tugged at her jeans, revealing the sweet curve of her buttock. Softly, he pressed his lips to her hip.

"It's lower," she said. "And more to the left."

Sam kissed her again. "There?"

"No, lower," she urged, trying to point with her finger.

He tugged her jeans down a bit more and brushed her hand aside. "How about here?" he asked. He touched her skin with his tongue and she stiffened. Slowly, he traced a trail with his lips to the small of her back, to the dimples that he'd found so intriguing.

"What are you doing?" she asked.

"Tending to your snakebite," he murmured.

She turned around and yanked her jeans up, regarding him suspiciously. "I wasn't bitten by a snake, was I?"

He smiled and shook his head. "Probably not. Maybe you just brushed up against a branch or an old thistle. It's so cold, the snakes are still a little sleepy. They hibernate over the winter and until the weather is warmer, they don't move around much. But it's better to be safe than sorry, don't you think?"

Sarah buttoned her jeans, sending him a withering look. "It might be nice if you teach me something about the wilderness instead of tormenting me with it."

He studied her for a moment, then nodded. It would give him something more to think about than the feel of her skin beneath his fingers. "All right. Let's see if you can make a fire. Any ideas?"

"Matches?" she said. "Cigarette lighter? Flame thrower?"

"In a survival situation, you'd be lucky to have any of those things. You'll usually find flint or a magnifying glass in a survival kit. But if you don't have matches or a survival kit, you can create an ember with friction."

Sam looked around the campsite for the materials he needed. After he gathered them, he laid them on the ground and asked Sarah to kneel there. He took his place behind her, wrapping his arms around her and resting his chin on her shoulder.

For a moment, he lost himself in the scent of her hair. He fought the urge to explore the curve of her neck, to press his lips to the soft skin beneath her ear. He closed his eyes and drew a deep breath.

"What are we doing here?" she asked. "Waiting for lightning to strike?"

"This is the fire-plow method," Sam explained, bringing his thoughts back to the lesson at hand. "You'll need two pieces of dry wood, a stick from a hardwood tree, like oak or maple and a trough from a softwood tree, like pine or birch. And you'll need tinder, dry grass, some small sticks, dry leaves. Just make sure everything's dry."

He showed her how to rub the stick back and forth

in the trough, moving faster and faster until the wood began to smoke. Holding her in his embrace, he couldn't help but realize just how erotic fire-making could be—all the movement and friction, the back and forth motion, the heat and the eventual ignition. Considering his near constant state of arousal around Sarah, Sam thought it was no wonder he'd managed get turned on by something as mundane as building a fire.

"It's getting hot," she said, her voice excited.

"Uh-huh." So was he. Sarah's backside kept bumping against his crotch, the contact becoming almost unbearable.

"How long do we have to do this?" she asked.

"Just keep going. Just like that. A nice quick tempo. There. Don't stop."

"Oh," she murmured. "I think it's coming. Look, look, a little ember."

Sam bit back a groan, trying to regain his composure and ignore his growing erection. "Drop some of the tinder on top of it," he said, "and then…just… blow."

"Blow," she repeated. She leaned forward, giving Sam a tempting view of her backside. "It's starting to catch."

"I bet it is," he murmured, his imagination taking flight. If she sat back very slowly and he shifted just slightly forward…his breath froze as an image flashed in his mind. That might be a very interesting position, he mused.

Suddenly, she sat back on her heels, sending his desire into overdrive. "Now what do I do?" Sarah asked.

Sam quickly scrambled to his feet. If he didn't put

some distance between them, he'd never be able to keep his hands off her. "Just add a little more fuel to the fire," he said. "You don't want to let it go out. I'll just get a bit more wood."

He wandered away from the campsite, wondering how he'd survive the next few days. He'd climbed mountains and rafted rivers and spent winters alone in the wilderness. But just the prospect of sleeping next to Sarah without making wild, crazy love to her was enough to make him seriously question his willpower.

The wilderness was a dangerous place and it was getting more dangerous with every minute he spent with Sarah Cantrell.

4

SARAH FINISHED UP the last of her coffee, then set the cup down near the fire. After a long day of hiking, every muscle in her body ached. She'd never been much for working out, but she'd always thought she was a pretty fit person.

"You'd better turn in," Charlie said. "We'll need to get an early start tomorrow."

"All right," Sarah said. She rose and dusted off the back of her jeans, then walked to the tent, stumbling slightly in the dark. She paused for a long moment, before stepping inside. "Are you coming?"

"Nah. I'm going to sleep out here by the fire."

Sarah gasped. "But it's freezing."

"I'll put a few more layers on. I'll be fine."

"No." Sarah walked back to the fire. "It's your tent, your sleeping bag. We can certainly share it. I promise I won't take advantage of you." Though she knew sleeping next to Charlie would be uncomfortable, she wasn't about to admit she couldn't control her desire for him. She didn't always have to think about kissing him and touching him, teasing and caressing him. Oh boy.

"All right," he said. "I need to take care of the fire and string the food up. I'll be in in a few minutes."

Sarah nodded, then returned to the tent. She un-

zipped the flap, kicked off her shoes and crawled inside. The sleeping bag was spread out on the floor of
the tent, the ground lumpy beneath it. But she was
so tired, Sarah suspected she could fall asleep anywhere. She lay back and tugged her jacket around
her to ward off the chill.

A few minutes later, Charlie joined her, tucking
her shoes and his boots into the corner of the tent. He
closed the flap, then stretched out beside her in the
dark. Sarah noticed he was doing everything he
could to avoid making contact with her. For a man
who'd known her in the most intimate way, he certainly was acting skittish. The atmosphere inside the
tent crackled with tension, but Sarah wasn't about to
surrender to her desires. Two could play at this
game.

"My feet are freezing," she murmured.

Charlie rubbed his feet against hers, the friction
from his wool socks sending warmth through her
toes. "Better?"

She closed her eyes and sighed. "I'm beginning to
understand what you mean about life being simpler
out here," she murmured. "A few weeks ago, I was
worrying about budgets and production schedules.
And now, all I'm concerned about is how to keep my
feet warm."

Charlie rolled onto his side, facing her. Though
she couldn't see him, she could feel the heat of his
body next to hers. She wanted him to touch her, just
once, to reassure her that he still wanted her. Sarah
wasn't sure why it was so important to her, but it
was.

"You did well today. I was proud of you."

His sincere compliment warmed her more than a

blazing fire ever could. "I just put one foot in front of the other and kept moving," she said, "even though my feet were freezing and my legs were tired and that silly suitcase weighed a ton. But you know, I was living my life moment to moment without a thought for anything but the time when I could finally sit down." She heard him chuckle softly. "What?"

"You're a lot tougher than I thought you were."

"Not tough," she said, turning to face him. "Just stubborn." Sarah reached up and tugged at a strand of her hair, ticking his face with it. "It comes with the red hair."

Charlie reached over and gently smoothed his palm over her cheek, brushing her hair from her face and furrowing his fingers through it. "I like your hair." He leaned closer and dropped a kiss on her lips. "And your mouth." He dragged his thumb along her eyebrow. "And your eyes."

Sarah moved closer, her legs tangling with his, inviting him to draw her into a deeper kiss. But Charlie grabbed her waist and turned her around, pulling her up against him, tucking the curve of her backside into his lap. Then he pulled the edge of the sleeping bag over them both.

"Go to sleep, Sarah," he murmured.

She blinked, confused by his cool reaction. Had she done something wrong? She tried to pull away, but Charlie held her close, one arm around her waist, the other providing a pillow for her head. Sarah closed her eyes, but his proximity made it impossible for her to sleep. Tiny currents of desire raced through her every time he moved and the warmth of his breath on her nape made her pulse pound.

If she turned and kissed him again, would he slowly undress her and make love to her? Or would their one-night stand remain just that, a single night not to be repeated? She wriggled back against him, craving the heat from his body and praying for exhaustion to overwhelm her.

Only sleep would release her from this infatuation she had with him—at least for a time. She felt like a schoolgirl, all dizzy with excitement whenever he looked at her or touched her. She'd gone her whole life without ever completely surrendering to a man and now she was ready to relinquish every last bit of her power to him, just for another night of passion.

She wanted to let go with Charlie, to close her eyes and let her desire spiral out of control. With him, she felt safe. Sarah reached down and took his hand in hers, sliding it up under her jacket and sweater until his cold fingers pressed against her warm belly. He smoothed his palm along her waist, the gentle caress making her skin tingle.

At first, his touch relaxed her. But then, she needed more. She arched back against him, weaving her fingers through his and guiding his hand higher, from her stomach to her breast.

His breath caught and then he nuzzled her neck, kissing the skin beneath her ear. He seemed to know what she needed, yet he waited for her invitation to take more. Didn't he know how much she wanted him? His thumb teased her nipple through the silky fabric of her bra and Sarah moaned.

It was simple, this desire between them, stripped of any pretense. He touched her, she responded, she touched him and he responded, and it would continue until neither one of them could stop. But she should want to stop, shouldn't she? Sarah knew the risk she took allowing herself to let passion overwhelm her sense of self-preservation.

If she let this go on, sooner or later, she wouldn't be able walk away. She'd convince herself she was in love with this man, that she couldn't live without him, that they were meant to be together.

Heat pulsed through her veins, chasing away the chill of the day and making her even sleepier. His hand drifted down to the waistband of her jeans and he worked at the button, then slid the zipper down.

Sarah held her breath as he ran his palm along her hip. How was it that this felt so right between them? The moment his hands possessed her, every doubt vanished. And yet they'd known each other for only two days. There were men she'd dated for months who had never managed to take her beyond her own insecurities.

She felt herself lulled and then he moved again, drawing her body back against him, his hand sliding to her lower abdomen. Suddenly, she was wide-awake, aware that he'd wandered into not-so-innocent territory. She pushed his hand lower, craving the sweet release that his touch promised.

"Please," she murmured.

His breath was soft and warm against her ear as he began to stroke her. "Is this what you want?"

"Yes. Yes."

He knew exactly how to minister to her, how gently, how slowly. Tiny currents of pleasure shot through her, gathering at her core until every nerve in her body felt on fire. Sarah shifted, allowing him to slip his finger inside of her.

Her breath stilled as she fought against her surrender. But then she realized it was useless to resist. Charlie owned her body and he was slowly taking possession of her soul as well.

The orgasm struck her suddenly, her body spasming, a tiny cry slipping from her throat. He continued to stroke her, softly now, drawing the last shudder from deep inside her. And then, a lovely exhaustion settled over her, every muscle loose and every nerve humming.

He'd been right. Life was simple when it was re-duced to elemental needs—thirst, hunger, warmth, rest…and, yes, sexual release. But it was only simple here, away from the real world.

"Go to sleep, Sarah," he murmured again, kissing the back of her neck.

Grabbing his hand, she drew it up and held it against her heart. She closed her eyes and knew the next time she opened them, the sun would be up. And she'd have another day—and maybe one more night—with Charlie.

Only after that would she worry about how she'd stop needing him.

SARAH WOKE just after dawn. Charlie was moving around the tent, trying to avoid waking her, but when he saw her watching him, he leaned over and kissed her.

"Morning," he said, his mouth lingering over hers.

"Is it?" She pushed up on her elbow. Every mus-cle in her body ached, her nose was freezing and she desperately needed a toothbrush. "What are you doing?"

He held up a gray vinyl bag. "I'm going to go

fetch some water. There's a stream about a quarter mile down the trail. I'll be back in a bit."

"I'll come with you," Sarah said.

"No, sleep in. Stay warm. I'll get breakfast ready and you can get up later."

Sarah smoothed her hands over the down sleeping bag. "I thought I was supposed to be carrying my own weight on this trip."

He chuckled, then handed her a silver whistle. "If you see a bear, use this. If you don't want to see a bear, stay in the tent."

Sarah took the whistle from his fingers and slipped it around her neck. "Got it, Chief." She gave him a weak salute, then flopped back down.

He stepped out of the tent, zipping it up behind him. Sarah stared at the simple framework of poles that held up the tent. She was almost glad for the time alone. When Charlie was around, it was difficult to focus on the task at hand.

She'd come to Sutter Gap with one goal in mind, to find Sam Morgan. And here she was, starting fires with sticks, sleeping on the ground and sharing a tent with a man who made her crazy with need. In the past twenty-four hours, she'd spent just a few minutes thinking about work and the balance of her time thinking about Charlie Wilbury.

Where was she supposed to go from here? Once Charlie took her to Sam, would all of this be over? Would she present her proposal, get her answer and then go on with her life?

He'd ruined her for any other man. Sarah couldn't imagine dating without making the comparisons to Charlie, both in and outside the bedroom. And even now, she knew she'd never feel this kind of desire again.

There had to be a way to keep him in her life for a little longer. If Sam agreed to do the program, perhaps she could hire Charlie as a consultant or a producer. At least then she'd have an excuse to see him occasionally.

Sarah rolled over on her stomach and sighed. This was crazy. Their one-night stand had turned into a two-night stand. And there was every chance that they'd add a few more nights before she went back to Belfort. But she had to be honest with herself. Though being with Charlie was exciting and exhilarating, it shouldn't have lasted more than a single night.

She sat up and tossed the sleeping bag aside, then combed her fingers through her tangled hair. If she expected to get out of this unscathed, then she'd have to keep reminding herself she had a life outside the wilderness and stop panting after Charlie.

Sarah grabbed her shoes and tugged them on, ignoring the laces. Charlie had rebuilt the fire and the damp wood hissed in the morning silence. She wandered over and held her hands out to the warmth, then glanced around for his backpack. She could at least comb her hair and brush her teeth before he returned.

He'd tied the pack to a high branch, the rope secured around the trunk of the tree. Sarah worked at the knot, then slowly lowered it to the ground. After she dragged it over to the fire, she found her cosmetics bag tucked in beside her underwear and Charlie's wallet. She grabbed the bag and then at the last minute took his wallet as well.

Sarah knew she shouldn't snoop, but her curiosity got the better of her. Had he refilled his supply of condoms? He'd never intended for her to come on this trip and if he hadn't brought any protection along, then she'd have an excuse for staying out of his bed.

She glanced around, listening carefully for approaching footsteps. Then she quickly opened his wallet and rifled through the contents. To her disappointment, she found no condoms tucked in with the paper money. Sarah shoved her fingers into the pockets that held his credit cards and driver's license. But there were no foil packets to be found.

Disappointed, she pulled out his driver's license and examined the photograph. Her license photo looked as if she'd just come off a three-week bender. Charlie's looked like it had been taken for the cover of a men's magazine, all windblown hair, suntanned face and perfect smile.

She glanced at his birthday, but as she did, her gaze skimmed across the name. Sarah blinked, confused by what she saw. "Samuel J. Morgan," she murmured. "178 Riverside Drive, New York, New York." She pinched her eyes closed and opened them again, certain she'd misread the name. But there it was—Samuel J. Morgan with a picture of Charlie Wilbury next to the name.

Sarah considered all the possible explanations. Charlie had stolen Sam Morgan's driver's license and pasted his own picture onto it. Maybe he was cashing the man's checks illegally. Or he'd murdered Sam Morgan and assumed his identity. Sarah sat down on the damp ground, staring at the license and trying to make sense of it all.

There was one explanation that was much simpler—the man she knew as Charlie Wilbury was really Sam Morgan. Sarah groaned. It made perfect sense. Her mind spun back through their conversations. He'd been so sure Sam wouldn't agree to her proposal, he'd insisted she'd be wasting her time and he'd done what he could to keep her from following him up the mountain. And if that wasn't enough, he could almost find his way to Sam's cabin with his eyes closed.

"Oh, you are such an idiot," Sarah muttered, anger surging up inside her. Why had she ever trusted him? He'd been lying to her all along, hiding from her in plain sight.

It's no wonder he'd fooled her. She'd been so befuddled by her attraction to him, she hadn't seen the truth. He could have told her he was the prime minister of Paraguay and she'd have believed him!

This was exactly what she should have expected from him. After all he'd already lied to her once, leaving her behind in Sutter Gap when he'd promised to take her up the mountain. And now he'd lied to her again. What else was he hiding from her?

Sarah snatched up the whistle and blew it over and over again, the piercing sounding breaking the silence of the woods. This was an emergency bigger than bears or squirrels or anything else the woods might produce. She'd just stumbled across a really nasty snake.

A few seconds later, she heard Sam crashing through the bushes. She shoved the wallet back into his pack and then waited. When he appeared, he had a frantic look on his face. He glanced around the campsite, breathless, his hands braced on his knees. "What was it?" he gasped. "Bear?"

"Snake," she muttered.

He frowned. "Snake? Are you sure? It's too cold for snakes."

"Really? It wasn't too cold for one of them to go after my butt yesterday."

He looked around again. "I guess it's gone now?"

She pushed to her feet. "I don't know—snakes can be pretty sneaky." She picked up her sweater and shook it out. "I can't believe how cold it is this morning. I hope you don't mind—I brought your pack down."

Sam sent her a wary look. "I expected you'd still be sleeping." He set the bag of water he'd retrieved near the fire. "Are you hungry?"

"Famished," Sarah muttered. She wanted to scream at him, to demand an explanation. Just what had he hoped to achieve by lying to her, besides making her look like a complete and utter fool?

"Are you all right?"

"Sure, I'm fine." Sarah toyed with the buttons on her sweater, trying to decide exactly how she wanted to handle the situation. Had they been in a steeper section of the mountain, she might have just given him a little shove. Or she could find an accommodating bear who'd agree to make a meal out of Sam. But maybe there was a way to make him squirm for a while. "I was just thinking about Sam Morgan."

She saw the subtle shift in his expression. He was curious, but he couldn't act too curious. "Are you worried he's not going to listen to your proposal?"

"No. I was still wondering, what would make a guy disappear into the wilderness? I know you said it was the solitude. But there has to be more to it."

"Like what?"

"Maybe it's some kind of sexual problem. Think about it. He's up here all alone, no women for miles. Don't you think he'd get…horny? Or maybe he's too crazy to get horny. Maybe he's one of those delusional paranoid psychotics. You know, the kind of guy who thinks that government agents go around implanting microchips in everyone's head. The kind who believe aliens are among us. Or maybe he can't live in society because he's dangerous. Maybe he robs old ladies or kidnaps children or sleeps with sheep." She looked up at him in mock horror. "Do you think that's it? Does he keep any sheep at his cabin in the woods?"

Sam gave her an uneasy smile. "He's just a normal guy, Sarah."

"No," Sarah said, shaking her head. "He can't be normal. He's hiding something." She paused for dramatic effect. "He's got a secret and he's afraid if he's around people, they'll somehow find out. Maybe he's not who he says he is. Maybe he's somebody entirely different. He could have committed a crime."

"He's not a criminal."

"Well, he might still be dangerous. Or maybe he's a mob hit man in witness protection. Just how much do you really know about him?"

"Enough to know that he's not any of those things," Sam insisted.

"Well, I'm glad you're with me. Who knows what dangers might befall me if I was left alone in the wilderness with a psycho like Sam Morgan? You'll protect me, won't you? After all, that's what I'm paying you for, right?"

He stared at her for a long moment and Sarah wondered if he'd ever even considered telling her the

truth. How long did he intend to carry on this cha-
rade? Would he lie beside her again tonight, pretend-
ing to be someone he wasn't?

"You don't have anything to be afraid of." Sam
grabbed the bag of water and filled the coffeepot.
"Lesson number two—water. The spring runoff is
pretty clean, but it's always a good idea to boil the
water for twenty minutes if you're going to use it for
cooking or drinking."

"Good to know," Sarah said. She watched as he
added wood to the fire, preparing to cook breakfast
for them both. Maybe she ought to confront him
about his deception right away and demand that he
take her back to Sutter Gap. But she still couldn't forget her goal. Sam Morgan might be a snake, but he
was *her* snake, and the future star of *Wilderness*. She
couldn't act indignant until she was certain he'd agree
to sign on the dotted line. Because, despite how much
she despised him, she knew her business well enough
to understand that Sam the snake would be a hit.

She sat down near the fire and tucked her knees
up under her chin. Why hadn't he just admitted his
lie to her yesterday? He could have told her who he
was and sent her right back to Sutter Gap—unless he
was actually considering her proposal. But hope was
quickly dashed when she thought of a more logical
reason.

She didn't want to believe it was the sex, but Sarah
had no other options to consider. She might have
thought differently if Sam Morgan hadn't just spent
six months alone in the woods. One night with a
warm and willing woman was likely exactly what
he'd been looking for. And given the chance for two
or three nights, he'd grabbed at it.

She smiled to herself. "Let's see just how far he'll go to get me back into his sleeping bag," she murmured.

Sam turned around. "Did you say something?"

She smiled and shook her head. He might have survived three winters living in the wilderness, but he'd never be able to survive the next few days with her.

THE SNOW BEGAN shortly after they broke camp. Sam had felt it in the air, the damp wind gradually turning colder as the morning wore on. There was always the chance of snow in spring, especially in the higher elevations. And had he been alone, it might not have bothered him.

But Sarah was already struggling with the climb, her face rosy from the cold and her breath coming in tiny gasps. She hadn't brought a hat though the gloves and fleece pullover he'd given her to wear beneath her jacket seemed to help. She was comfortable for the moment. But if the weather got worse, the rest of the hike could be treacherous.

He glanced over his shoulder and found her lagging behind, the bear whistle still dangling from her neck. She'd been oddly quiet since they'd set off, but he was fairly certain his explanations about black bear behavior had quelled any fears she might have on that subject. There had to be something else bothering her, besides her preoccupation with snakes.

His mind wandered back to the previous night, to the intimacies they'd shared in the tent. Lying beside her, exploring her, it had taken all his willpower not to make love to her. But what had begun as a tiny little lie had suddenly grown into a brick wall between them. The next time he made love to her, he wanted her to murmur the name Sam in the midst of her passion.

He slowed his pace, waiting for her to catch up to him, but she maintained her distance. Frustrated, Sam stood in the middle of the trail and she stopped, kicking at a tree root with the toe of her shoe. "We need to pick up the pace," he called.

"Fine," she shouted. "You know me, I'll believe whatever you tell me. You're the expert. Charlie Wilbury, wilderness guide. Lead the way, Charlie Wilbury."

Scowling, Sam walked back to where she'd stopped. She met his gaze and in that instant, he realized what the problem was. She knew the truth. He cursed inwardly. All right, now that it was out in the open, what was he supposed to do? He could pretend he didn't know she was on to him or he could admit the truth and face the consequences.

Sam considered his options for a few moments longer, then decided he had a third. He grabbed her arms, pulled her against his body and kissed her hard. When he was satisfied that the kiss had the desired effect, Sam stepped back and looked down into her flushed face. Her eyes slowly opened and he held out his hand. "Sam Morgan," he murmured. "Nice to meet you."

Sarah opened her mouth then snapped it shut. Anger flickered in her eyes. She drew a steady breath, her jaw tight. Then she shoved him hard, sending him stumbling backward. "You lied to me, you—you snake."

"You snooped in my wallet," he countered.

Sarah cursed. "Yes, I did."

"Good, I was hoping you would. And now that

we have this all cleared up, we need to keep moving."

"You think I'm going to continue on after this? I'm exhausted, I'm cold, I'm hungry, my feet hurt and I want to feed you to the bears. I'm not taking another step."

"All right. I'll give you five minutes. Go ahead, just let 'er rip. Tell me what an ass I am, how I took advantage of you, how you'd never have slept with me if you'd known the truth. But make it quick, because we have to keep moving."

"You—you are a…a…" Sarah cursed again, then spun on her heel and started back down the trail. When she'd retreated ten yards, she turned around. "You never had any intention of considering my proposal, did you?"

"I considered it," Sam said. "But I don't want my life turned into a television show."

"Why didn't you just say that? It would have saved us both a lot of time."

Sam didn't have an answer for her question, at least not one that made any sense. From the moment he'd met her, he'd been operating on instinct alone. He couldn't deny the attraction between them had been an influencing factor. He didn't want to deny it. Besides, she'd made it almost impossible to just walk away from her. She'd been the one to seduce him that first night, or at least she'd thrown the first kiss. How could you blame a guy for not turning away from that?

"Maybe I did lie," Sam admitted. "But we still would have spent an incredible night in bed. The attraction was mutual. I know it was. And what we shared in that motel room had nothing to do with

Sam Morgan and Sarah Cantrell. That was all about a man and a woman and a lot of great sex. You said so yourself, right? We were both adults and we knew what we were doing."

He watched as she tried to formulate a response.

"I never mix business with pleasure," she finally said.

"Would it make you feel better if I told you I'd already decided to turn down your proposal before I walked into your motel room? We were in the clear. As far as I was concerned, there was no business between us. You just didn't know about it."

"How can you say that? You haven't even listened to my proposal." She rummaged through his backpack and pulled out her laptop. "I have a good idea here. We could do this the right way. Just let me show you what I have planned, then give me your answer. If it's no, then I'll go back to Sutter Gap and leave you alone."

Just the thought of her walking away from him was enough to make his stomach twist into a knot. It couldn't be over so easily. There was something between them and he had to figure out exactly what it was and for that, he needed time. Sam shook his head. "I'm not going to listen to it, Sarah. And you aren't going back to Sutter Gap. Not today."

"You brought me here under false pretenses. If you don't have any intention of listening to my plan, then I'm not taking another step up this mountain." She crossed her arms over her chest and Sam knew it would be useless to argue the point. As Carter had said, Sarah Cantrell was powerful stubborn.

"All right," he said. "I'll listen to your plan."

She nodded, then knelt down, resting her laptop

on her knee. "I'm not sure how long my battery will last out here in the cold, so I'll just skip all the bells and whistles and get right to the point."

"No," Sam said. "Not here. I'll listen once we get to my cabin."

"I want an answer right now," Sarah insisted.

"You have to learn to be more patient." Sam grabbed her laptop and snapped it shut then shoved it into his pack. "The weather is going bad on us. The wind is picking up and within the next hour, it's going to start snowing. I'd rather spend the night warm and safe in my cabin than cold and uncomfortable in a tent."

She studied him for a long moment, weighing the truth of his words, then finally nodded. "All right. But as soon as we get there, I'll make my presentation and you'll give me an answer. And then tomorrow, you'll take me back to Sutter Gap."

"Deal," he said. He stared up at the sky, now a dull gray. "We've got two more hours of hard hiking ahead of us."

"Don't think this means I forgive you for lying to me," she said.

"And don't think I'm going to say yes to your proposal because I feel guilty about lying to you." He pointed to a ridge high above them. "We're going up there."

She didn't lag behind this time. Instead, she stayed hard on his heels, sometimes bumping into him when he had to navigate a tricky section of the trail.

"You have to understand. I'm not interested in making some silly reality show," Sarah explained along the way. "It's going to have a documentary feel to it, like the *National Geographic* specials. And I want to tie it in to the pioneer history of our county, to show viewers what it was like for people to move into the wilderness and carve out a living. In the centuries past, thousands of families lived just like you, miles from cities and towns, totally dependent on what they could gather from the land, and I think that's an important point to make in today's society."

Sam cursed softly then turned on her. He grabbed her and brought his mouth down on hers, kissing her deeply. To his surprise, she didn't offer any resistance. He'd expected her to at least put up the pretense she was still angry with him. As forcefully as he grabbed her, he set her back. "Shut up," he said.

Sarah gasped. "What?"

"I said, shut up. When you talk you don't walk as fast. Until we get to the cabin, I want you to keep quiet. If you insist on speaking, then I'm going to have to take appropriate action—as I did just then."

He started off again, picking up his pace and trying to ignore the involuntary reaction happening in the area of his lap. It sure didn't take much. The power she held over him was inexplicable. Forget the possibility of snow. He ought to pitch the tent right here, drag Sarah inside and prove to her how incredible they were together.

How could she possibly argue the point? Last night, he'd made her shudder with desire, bringing her to release with just a few simple moves of his hand. It was an incredible feeling to have that kind of control over a woman's body. But with Sarah, it wasn't about power. It was about pleasing her, about making her want him as much as he wanted her.

A fallen tree blocked the trail and Sam crawled

over it then waited for Sarah. He took her hand and helped her over, taking the chance to admire her rosy cheeks and bright green eyes.

He'd never craved a woman the way he craved Sarah. And though he didn't yet understand his reasons for the depth of his need, he didn't question it. All that mattered was that she was sheer perfection, a crazy mix of beauty and intelligence and fire that he found irresistible. As long as she was near, he was happy.

Whenever he looked her, he saw the passionate Sarah lying beneath him that night at the Gap View, her auburn hair spread across the pillow, her eyes closed, her lips parted. And he saw the stubborn Sarah sitting on her suitcase in the middle of the road, and the indignant Sarah fuming over the lie he'd told. It didn't matter which woman she was, he was captivated by them all.

When he'd walked off the mountain a few days ago, Sam had been a free man without a care in the world except where he could find a good meal, a hot shower and no-strings sex. But now he found himself walking back up the mountain with a woman who managed to tie him into so many knots he wasn't sure he'd ever escape.

5

THE CABIN WAS exactly as Sarah had imagined it. She caught sight of it through the leafless trees as they climbed the final fifty yards of a well-worn trail. The exterior was made of hand-hewn logs and the wood-shingled roof was edged with rough wooden gutters that lead to a rain barrel at one corner. Firewood was piled neatly against the house on the south side and an iron pot hung over a fire pit in a small clearing to the north. She couldn't imagine how Sam had managed to build the little home all alone.

"It's perfect," she said, staring at it in awe.

"Is that the producer talking?" Sam asked.

"It's amazing," Sarah admitted. "I'm impressed. It looks just like a real log cabin."

"It *is* a real log cabin." He took her hand and led her up to the front door. "Come on, I'll show you around."

It felt good to have him touch her again, Sarah mused. Even after all he'd done, after all her rage, she still wanted him. The entire way up the mountain, she'd wondered about the man Sam Morgan was. And when she'd learned the truth, it hadn't really surprised her. Sam Morgan, Charlie Wilbury, he was still the man she'd made love to. She'd never known anyone quite like him, so focused and determined, so strong yet so enigmatic.

Even if she walked away from him tomorrow, it would be a long time before she'd forget the thrill of his touch or the taste of his mouth or the way he whispered her name when he was inside her. Months from now, she'd try to recall everything that had happened between them and it would still be there. No, a woman didn't easily forget a man like Sam Morgan.

"When I decided to build the cabin, I wanted to do it the traditional, old-fashioned way," he explained. "I only used tools that were available in the early 1800s."

Sarah nodded, barely listening to his words. She was transfixed by his gaze. Out here in the wilderness, everything seemed more intense—the blue of his eyes, the solid strength of his body, the warmth of his smile. "Wait," she said. She searched her jacket pockets for her BlackBerry and when she found it, she flipped it on. "I want to take notes."

Sam snatched the PDA from her hand, shaking his head. "If you want to take notes, I have pencils and paper inside. We don't use modern conveniences on this mountain."

"All right," Sarah said, accepting the challenge. "Go ahead, tell me more. I'll write it down later."

"It's amazing what can be done with a few simple tools and a lot of patience," Sam continued. "I remember sitting in science class when I was kid, learning about levers and pulleys and thinking, I'm never going to use this. And then it became the most important thing I knew. I'm planning to write Miss Rockwell and thank her."

"Miss Rockwell?"

"My eighth grade science teacher." He grinned.

"To a geek like me, she was the closest thing to heaven. And she looked great in safety goggles." His eyes skimmed over her face. "You'd probably look great in goggles, too."

"Don't try to charm me," Sarah warned. "It won't work this time."

He turned to her, pressing her hands between his and staring down into her face. "What will work, Sarah? Will you accept my apology? Because I am sorry. I truly am."

His gaze drifted down to her mouth and she held her breath. If he kissed her now, she'd be lost. Every nerve in her body cried out for him, for the promise of release that she'd experienced with his hands and his body. She swallowed hard. "Show me the cabin."

He nodded. "It's a little rough," he said as he opened the door. "Spartan might be a better word for it. They don't deliver furniture this far out so I had to make most of what I have. And there's no electricity or running water, so you'll have to make adjustments. I get water from a stream or the rain barrel. There's an outhouse in back. And there's a bed. I sewed the mattress myself. I made it out of corn-husks from corn I grew."

A few moments later, Sam struck a match and lit an oil lamp. The lamp cast everything in a soft, almost romantic glow. Sarah turned a slow circle, examining every detail. It wasn't much larger than her bedroom at home. It looked exactly like a pioneer cabin, from the wooden pegs on the wall that held his clothes to the washbowl and pitcher on a table near the window to the rough plank table in the center of the room.

"Why don't you make yourself at home?" he said. "I'll make a fire."

Sarah nodded, then sat down on the edge of his bed, the mattress crunching beneath her. She tugged off her muddy shoes and, tucking her feet up beneath her, watched as he hauled armloads of wood inside.

He'd been right. The attraction between them had been undeniable. Even if she had known who he was, she probably would have done exactly the same thing. This whole idea of separating business from pleasure only really counted back in Charleston, right? The rules were different here in the wilderness.

Soon, a blazing fire crackled in the hearth. Sarah was amazed how quickly the cabin warmed up. Sam swung a pot of water over the flames and when it had warmed he carried it to the side of the bed.

"What's that for?" she asked.

"Your feet. Just because we're living in the middle of nowhere, doesn't mean we can't enjoy a few luxuries."

Sarah dangled her legs over the edge of the bed and Sam removed her socks. Her feet were red and blistered and they ached with the cold. Gently, he smoothed his warm, wet hands over them, massaging until the circulation had been restored.

Sarah moaned softly. She'd never realized her feet were an erogenous zone. Or maybe Sam had turned them into one. What other parts of her body were just waiting to be transformed by his touch? Her kneecaps? Her left armpit? Suddenly, Sarah wanted to know.

She'd tried to keep herself from fantasizing about him, from creating a future that she knew they'd never have. Sarah had decided long ago that the traditional roles that women took were not for her. She wouldn't make a good wife. The thought of pledging her devotion to just one man struck fear into her heart. If she allowed herself the luxury of loving, then she opened herself to all the risks, including losing a man who'd become her whole life.

Sam drew her foot up and pressed a kiss into the arch. "Why don't you make yourself more comfortable?" he suggested. "I have some clean clothes you can wear. Yours are a bit damp." He retrieved a hooded sweatshirt and a pair of sweatpants from a crate beneath the bed then handed them to her. "I know they're not very flattering, but on a cold night, they make cozy pajamas."

"Thanks," Sarah said. She set the clothes beside her on the bed, waiting for an opportunity to change in privacy. Just hours ago, she wouldn't have bothered. But the rules had changed and she had to be more cautious now.

Sam's eyebrow cocked up. "Are you just going to sit there in your wet clothes?"

"I'll change later," she said. "I'm fine."

He shook his head then grabbed her hands, pulling her to her feet. He quickly removed her jacket and tugged her sweater over her head. "You're going to have to learn to be more practical, Sarah. This cabin has one room and no privacy. Besides, I've already seen you naked. I can handle it."

He grabbed the hem of her turtleneck, but Sarah pushed his hands away. Could he handle it? More to the point, could she handle him stripping the clothes off her body? Sarah slowly pulled the turtleneck up along her torso and then, in a deliberately provocative movement, drew it over her head.

When she looked at Sam, she instantly read his expression. Desire flickered in his gaze as his eyes skimmed over her body. She unbuttoned her jeans and shimmied out of them, kicking them aside. His fingers clenched and Sarah smiled inwardly. He was thinking about putting his hands on.

"You're gorgeous," he murmured, his gaze drifting over her body.

His simple words sent a shiver skittering over her skin and she grabbed the sweatshirt and pulled it over her head, then quickly tugged on the sweatpants. Drawn by the warmth, Sarah crossed to the fireplace and held her hands out to the flames.

Sarah could feel his eyes on her. Goose bumps prickled her flesh. It wasn't from the cold, but the anticipation. Everything had seemed so straightforward when it had been all about lust. But Sarah sensed there was something more going on between them, something much more intense just below the surface. She wanted physical contact with him, but not for the ultimate release he could give her. She wanted the warmth and affection and security that his touch gave her.

"Why don't you pull that rocker up to the fire?" he suggested. "I'm going to make us some dinner."

As she watched Sam move around the cabin, Sarah realized how utterly alone they were. If things got difficult or even unbearable between them, there would be no escape. All alone with a man who made her heart pound and her body tremble with need. Sarah was more scared of what might happen inside the cabin than the dangers that lurked outside.

There was only one bed. Would they share it? And if they did, would what had transpired last night happen again? Curling up in the rocking chair, she let exhaustion claim her. Sarah felt herself drifting, the warmth of the fire making her sleepy.

The next thing she knew, Sam was whispering her name. She opened her eyes and saw him bent over the rocker, his hands braced on the arms.

Sarah yawned. "I fell asleep," she murmured.

"You did," he replied. He bent closer and an instant later, his lips touched hers. Sarah felt light-headed, dizzy with the sensations rushing through her body. Kissing Sam seemed like the most natural thing in the world, as if it were merely the way they communicated and not the first step in seduction.

She parted her lips and her tongue danced against his, the kiss deepening until it became a sensual exploration. He reached out and cupped her cheek in his palm, urging her to give him more.

In that moment, he could have carried her to the bed and made love to her and she wouldn't have resisted. She ached to feel his weight on top of her, to feel his hips nestled between her legs as he moved inside her. He was hers and she was his, at least for the time that passed inside this cabin.

And though it wasn't a real commitment, or even a real relationship, it was the most Sarah had ever offered a man. For as long as they were here, she'd allow herself to want him and to need him. She'd give herself the freedom to enjoy what they'd shared, the intimacy and the vulnerability and everything that went with it.

For now, there'd be no future and no past, just the present. As his tongue teased at hers, Sarah gave herself over, allowing her mind to wander where it would—along the path of seduction. She wanted to unbutton his shirt, to press her lips to his bare skin, to run her hand beneath the waistband of his jeans. She knew the effect she had on his body and she wanted to incite his desire as he did hers.

When Sam drew back, Sarah opened her eyes again. Her gaze fell to his mouth, damp from their kiss. "I don't want to stop."

"I don't either," he murmured. He took her hands and drew her to her feet. "Come on. It's time for dinner. After we eat, I want to listen to your presentation."

Sarah frowned as he followed him to the table. In truth, she'd forgotten all about her presentation. Whether Sam listened to her proposal or not wouldn't change one important fact—tonight, she'd share his bed and she wouldn't hold anything back. For now, Sarah Cantrell belonged to Sam Morgan.

THE REMAINS of their meal lay spread across the plank table. Sarah glanced up at Sam and smiled sleepily. "Dinner was wonderful."

Sam watched her, enjoying the sight of her sitting at his table, dressed in his clothes, warmed by a fire he'd built. Odd how he took so much more satisfaction from simple tasks when they made her more comfortable. "It's not steak and wine, but you learn to enjoy what you have."

She reached for a tiny carved bird that sat on the center of the table and examined it carefully.

"Don't look too closely," he said. "I still haven't perfected my wood-carving technique."

A look of surprise suffused her face. "Did you make this?"

Sam nodded. "When the weather is bad, I have a lot of spare time on my hands. That was about my tenth or eleventh try. The first attempts didn't look like birds."

"It's really quite good," Sarah said. She drew her feet up and tucked her knees beneath her chin, then fixed her gaze on his. "So what do you do when the weather is good?"

"I usually take care of the business of living— hunting, fishing, searching for food. But sometimes I go out exploring. A couple years back, I found the remains of an old log cabin nearby. There were apple trees planted all around it and those apples—it was as if I'd discovered treasure. I hauled a ton of them back here and tried to figure out what to do with them all."

"Don't tell me you made pies. It took my friend Libby nearly three years to teach me how to make a decent piecrust and even now, I fail more than I succeed."

"Nope." He grinned. "I made booze. Carter brought me an old apple press and I made apple jack. It's like apple brandy. Would you like some?"

"Sure."

Sam fetched a jug and poured a good measure of the brandy into a tin cup, then handed it to her. She took a sip and then closed her eyes.

"It's good," she murmured. Drawing in a deep breath, she tipped her head back. "Do you ever get frightened being out here all alone? Don't you ever worry that something might happen and you won't be able to get help?"

"No," Sam said. That wasn't entirely true, he realized. He'd been a bit edgy since they'd arrived. "Not when I'm alone," he added.

"I scare you?" she asked.

"I'm just not used to being responsible for another person," he explained. "It's always been just me. And once in a while Carter comes up here for a day or two. But he can handle himself in the woods."

"Well, I'm hoping you'll be glad you brought me here. Will you listen to my ideas now?" she asked. "I think once you see what I'd like to do you might find it a really interesting project."

It was becoming more difficult to refuse Sarah anything. He found himself constantly looking for ways to make her happy, a warm soak for her feet, comfortable clothes, a tasty dinner. He couldn't refuse to take the time to listen. "You have to understand what this place means to me. Once you make it famous, there are going to be people trampling all over this mountain to find it."

"Then you've already decided," she said with a frown. "Try to have an open mind. Then, if you turn me down, I'll understand."

"All right. Go ahead. Get your computer and we'll see what you have planned."

Sarah smiled then hopped up from the table. "You won't be disappointed, I promise." She grabbed her laptop from a small table near the door and sat down next to him.

As she began to lay out her plans, Sam found himself captivated by the sound of her voice. She could read him the phone book and he'd find it fascinating—the Southern drawl she tried so hard to hide, the funny way she changed her train of thought midsentence, the way she answered her own rhetorical questions.

The program she'd put together on her computer was slick, filled with interesting graphics and concise marketing data. But he could barely concentrate on the presentation. He suddenly found himself almost considering her idea. After all, he'd never planned to stay in the wilderness forever.

For whatever reason, Sarah had him pondering the idea of going back to the real world. He'd always thought he'd make the decision for different reasons. He hadn't expected a woman might make it for him.

Did he actually believe he could have a future with Sarah? Or was he letting his physical desires affect his common sense? He'd spent months in this cabin alone without ever thinking about bringing a woman into his life. Then, from the first moment he'd touched Sarah, he couldn't think about anything else.

Maybe it was just nature's way of telling him there was more to life than the four walls of his cabin. There was the sweet curve of a woman's back, her soft sigh in the dark and the wonderful sensation of sinking into her heat. Of course, he'd enjoyed these pleasures fleetingly with other women, but with Sarah, the experience was so much more than just physical delight...it made him rethink the way he lived his life.

"So how do you like it so far?" Sarah asked.

Sam blinked, focusing again on the computer screen. "It's a plan," he said.

"Is that all you have to say?"

He closed his eyes and rubbed his forehead, trying to find the right way to explain. "This place is...sacred to me. It's part of who I am and I'm not sure I want to share it."

"You're sharing it with me," she said.

"You're different."

"Why?"

"I haven't figured that out yet," he said, frustration creeping into his voice. Why had he been so anxious to have her here? Was it just the prospect of spending more time with Sarah? Or did his reasons run much deeper? "Maybe I just didn't want to be alone right now."

"So, it really isn't me. It could have been any woman," she said.

Sam shook his head. "No. It was you. It was only you, I know that for sure."

She frowned, as if she wasn't sure how to take his explanation. Then she reached out and switched off her computer. "So, I guess I still don't have an answer." She drew a deep breath. "You know, we wouldn't have to tape here. We could find an entirely different location. Build a new cabin, start from the very beginning, just like you did three years ago. It's not this place that's important, it's you."

"All right," Sam relented. "I'll think about it. I promise, I will."

She closed her laptop and smoothed her hand over the top. "Why did you come here?"

"I just did," he said. Sam had never tried to explain his reasons. No one had ever bothered to ask. He probably would have been better off seeing a shrink rather than walking into the wilderness, but he'd never wanted to admit that he couldn't solve his own problems or heal his own pain. Maybe it was time to let it go, to say it all out loud.

"A friend of mine died a few years ago and it shook me up. I couldn't deal with it, so I came up here to get my head straight. I just never felt the need to go back."

"What was his name?" Sarah asked.

"Jeff Warren. He and I were best friends. We met as college roommates. My mom died when I was pretty young and then my dad the year before I began college. Jeff's family took me in. I stayed with them over the holidays and during the summer. We found summer jobs together, saved our money and traveled when we could. Jeff was like a brother."

"How did he die?" Sarah asked.

"After college, we both got jobs on Wall Street and started making some decent cash. We continued traveling together, but we were always looking for bigger and better adventures. We fed off all the adrenaline. We'd gone skydiving and bungee jumping and back-country skiing and scuba diving. We climbed rock faces and explored caves."

"That sounds dangerous," Sarah commented.

"It was. It was the only thing that made me feel alive." He paused. "That, and risking my clients' money in the stock market. I guess I just wanted to feel something." Sam sighed. "We had just climbed Mt. McKinley and were on our way down when we got hit by an avalanche."

Sarah gasped and reached for his hand. Her touch gave him the reassurance he needed to continue. Now that he'd begun, he wanted to say it all.

"Jeff got swept away and I managed to get out of the worst of the slide. One minute he was there and the next he was gone." Sam paused, swallowing back a lump of emotion. "I crawled down and started digging, but I couldn't get to him. I wasn't even sure where he was. I was so scared he'd be dead, and after a few hours of digging, I knew he was."

Sarah slowly stood, then reached down and smoothed her palm over his cheek. "I'm sorry," she said. "I'm sorry I said those things out on the trail."

Sam stared up into her eyes and found comfort there. He grabbed her around the waist and pulled her onto his lap, her thighs straddling his middle. Leaning into her, he pressed his face into her breasts, hugging her tightly.

"It was my fault," he said.

"How could it be your fault?"

"I just wanted to feel something."

Sarah ran her fingers through his hair and he closed his eyes, allowing himself to enjoy her touch. Then he stood and carried her to the fire, her legs still wrapped around his waist. He was already hard, his erection pressing against her with every step he took.

When he reached the warmth of the fire, he held Sarah against the rough wall beside the hearth and kissed her neck. "Why do I need you so much?" he murmured, confusion coloring his words.

Sarah tugged his head back and kissed him. "Do I make you feel something?"

He slid his hands up beneath her sweatshirt, desperate to feel her bare skin. "Yes," he murmured. She was so soft and warm, her curves made for his hands. He cupped her breast and when he teased at her nipple with his thumb, Sarah moaned softly. The sound sent a flood of need through his body.

"Tell me what you want," he murmured, his lips trailing from her ear to her throat. When she didn't answer, Sam pulled back. An uneasy expression clouded her pretty features. "What is it?"

Sarah shook her head. "Maybe we shouldn't do this. Not that I don't want to, because I do. But it's getting so complicated. And tomorrow, I'm going home and you'll come back here and our lives will be back to the way they were."

"What about your program?" he asked.

She smiled ruefully and brushed the hair out of his eyes. "Let's be honest. You don't have any intention of doing the program. And I don't blame you. I understand now and I think it's the right decision. But I've promised the station a new outdoor show for next season. If I don't deliver you, I'm going to be stuck producing *Billy Bob Barkley's Bass Fishing Bonanza.*"

Sam ran his thumb along her lower lip. She was right, things had turned complicated. At first, sex with Sarah had been all about satisfying a need. That's all he'd wanted from her. But now he'd begun to find comfort and understanding in the physical contact, an honesty that he'd never experienced with a woman before. If things went any further, Sam wasn't sure he'd be able to let her go.

He loosened his grip on her waist and she slid her legs down his thighs until she stood in front of him. "Maybe we should get some sleep," he said. "If the weather breaks, we'll go back down tomorrow."

She nodded. "I think that would be best." With that, she turned and walked to the bed. But when she got there, Sarah paused. "Where are you going to sleep?"

Sam had assumed he'd sleep in the bed with her. But now that didn't seem like a very good idea. "I'll just lie in front of the fire. And if you need to go to the outhouse, just wake me. I'll take you."

She glanced over her shoulder. "Good night, Sam."

"Good night, Sarah."

As she settled into his bed, he grabbed his sleeping bag and spread it across the floor. Then he kicked off his boots and shrugged out of his shirt. When he'd stretched out on the down bag, he glanced over at Sarah. "It was a good proposal," he said. "Just not for me."

"I understand," she murmured.

Sarah turned her back to him and tugged the wool blankets up around her shoulders. He closed his eyes and listened to her soft breathing, picturing himself beside her. His fingers tingled as he imagined smoothing his palm over her belly, running his hand up her thigh, exploring every sweet curve of her body.

Sam rolled to face the fire and stared into the flames. He didn't want to believe he'd never touch her again. But maybe it was time to start convincing himself that he didn't need her as much as he thought he did.

She was just a woman and there were plenty of other women in the world.

THE CABIN was so cold Sarah's breath clouded in front of her face. She pushed up on her elbow, her surroundings glowing with the faint light from the dying fire. Sam was sound asleep on the floor, dressed in just his jeans, the sleeping bag tossed aside. The corn-husk mattress crunched as she carefully crawled out of bed.

Outside, the wind howled and drafts of cold air pushed through the cracks beneath the door and around the tiny darkened windows. She wrapped the blanket around herself and tiptoed over to the fireplace.

Bending down, Sarah studied Sam as he slept. His features, usually so strong and angular, now appeared almost boyish—long dark lashes against his tanned skin, hair carelessly mussed and falling into his eyes, lips slightly curled in a sleepy smile. She reached out to touch him, but then thought better of it.

In many ways he was the strongest man she'd ever known, so determined and competent. But that tough exterior hid a wounded soul and Sarah wasn't sure she knew how to heal him. She'd never allowed herself to get so close to a man, to scratch away at the surface and find out what was beneath. That would have required a commitment on her part, something she'd been unwilling to give.

Sarah closed her eyes. He made her feel things she'd never felt before and it both fascinated and frightened her. She'd become desperate for his touch, yet she craved his respect and his affection as well.

She drew a ragged breath and turned to the fire, hoping to warm herself with something other than desire. But the embers were nearly dead and there was no wood left to stoke the flames. Cursing softly, Sarah stood and crossed back to the bed, then tugged on her shoes. The woodpile was just around the side of the house. If she drove away the chill, perhaps she could put her desire aside and sleep.

She grabbed her jacket and slipped it on. When she opened the door, the wind caught it and it swung open, sending a frigid blast through the cabin. Grabbing the iron handle, Sarah quickly pulled the door shut behind her.

The snow pelted her face and she drew her collar up to her ears and made her way along the front

wall of the cabin. There was no porch light to guide
her and the moon was obscured by storm clouds. It
was so dark she might as well have been blind, feeling her way along the log facade. She tried to count
her steps, knowing the distance she had to cover was
less than ten feet.

The snow was piled in drifts up to her knees and
by the time she reached the corner her feet were
already numb. Squinting into the darkness, Sarah
made the turn but something caught her foot and
stumbled forward.

Suddenly, she was face-down in the snow, the cold
hitting her skin like a million tiny pinpricks. She
struggled to her feet and brushed the snow out of her
eyes with stiff fingers. Then she reached out for the
cabin wall...but it wasn't there.

A wave of panic raced through her and Sarah
tried to calm herself. The cabin had been right beside her just a few seconds ago and it certainly
hadn't moved. She'd just lost her bearings.
"Relax," she murmured. "Just don't take a step
until you're sure."

She held her hands out in front of her and took
three careful steps, but all she could feel was empty
space. Sarah turned around and walked back to
where she started from, then took another three steps
in the opposite direction. But again, she ran into
nothing but cold and wind. "I must be walking par-
allel to the cabin," she murmured.

But as she tried to find her way, she began to tremble from a mixture of cold and fear and self-doubt.
What if she couldn't get back inside? What if she
had to spend the entire night in the snow and cold?
Why hadn't she thought to take a flashlight or a

GET FREE BOOKS and a FREE GIFT WHEN YOU PLAY THE...

Lucky 7

777

Just scratch off the silver box with a coin. Then check below to see the gifts you get!

SLOT MACHINE GAME!

YES! I have scratched off the silver box. Please send me the 2 free Harlequin Blaze™ books and gift for which I qualify. I understand I am under no obligation to purchase any books, as explained on the back of this card.

350 HDL D7W4　　　　　　　　　　　　**150 HDL D7XJ**

FIRST NAME　　　　　　　　　　LAST NAME

ADDRESS

APT.#　　　　CITY

STATE/PROV.　　　ZIP/POSTAL CODE

7	7	7
🍒	🍒	🍒
♣	♣	♣
🔔	🔔	🍒

Worth TWO FREE BOOKS plus a BONUS Mystery Gift!

Worth TWO FREE BOOKS!

Worth ONE FREE BOOK!

TRY AGAIN!

www.eHarlequin.com

(H-B-04/05)

DETACH AND MAIL CARD TODAY!

The Harlequin Reader Service® — Here's how it works:

Accepting your 2 free books and gift places you under no obligation to buy anything. You may keep the books and gift and return the shipping statement marked "cancel." If you do not cancel, about a month later we'll send you 4 additional books and bill you just $3.99 each in the U.S., or $4.47 each in Canada, plus 25¢ shipping & handling per book and applicable taxes if any.* That's the complete price and — compared to cover prices of $4.75 each in the U.S. and $5.75 each in Canada — it's quite a bargain! You may cancel at any time, but if you choose to continue, every month we'll send you 4 more books, which you may either purchase at the discount price or return to us and cancel your subscription.

*Terms and prices subject to change without notice. Sales tax applicable in N.Y. Canadian residents will be charged applicable provincial taxes and GST. Credit or debit balances in a customer's account(s) may be offset by any other outstanding balance owed by or to the customer.

If offer card is missing write to: Harlequin Reader Service, 3010 Walden Ave., P.O. Box 1867, Buffalo NY 14240-1867

BUSINESS REPLY MAIL

FIRST-CLASS MAIL   PERMIT NO. 717-003   BUFFALO, NY

POSTAGE WILL BE PAID BY ADDRESSEE

HARLEQUIN READER SERVICE
3010 WALDEN AVE
PO BOX 1867
BUFFALO NY 14240-9952

NO POSTAGE
NECESSARY
IF MAILED
IN THE
UNITED STATES

lantern? Surely, Sam would wake up any moment and come looking for her...wouldn't he?

Sarah pulled her hands up into the sleeves of her jacket. "Sam!" she shouted. "Help!" But her voice was lost in the howling wind.

She turned to her right and walked another three steps, then walked back six. Why couldn't she find her way? For all she knew, she was standing just a few feet from the cabin, but she was afraid to move anymore. "Sam!"

A faint voice came out of the dark. "Sarah?"

"Sam, I'm here."

A few moments later, she felt his hand on her shoulder. He grabbed her around the waist and drew her against him. "What the hell are you doing out here?"

Tears of relief trickled down her cheeks, the wind turning them to ice as they fell. "I—I was getting wood for the fire. But right now, I think I'm freezing to death."

He pulled her along and just a few short steps later, they were at the front door. Sam helped her inside, then quickly tore off her coat and drew her into his embrace, his hands frantically smoothing over her body. He rubbed her back, trying to warm her.

Sarah felt more tears pressing at the corners of her eyes. It was silly to cry, but she'd never been quite so scared before—or so grateful to find herself in a man's arms. How could something as simple as fetching wood turn so frightening? "It was pitch-black. I lost my bearings."

He grabbed her upper arms and set her back on her heels, his gaze searching hers, his expression tight. "Why the hell didn't you wake me? I could have gone out and gotten wood for you. Don't ever scare me like that again."

Sarah gasped at the anger in his tone. "Scare you? What about me?"

Sam led her over to the fire and sat her down in the rocking chair. "What if I hadn't come for you?" He tugged off her shoes and socks then began to rub her cold feet. "You're lucky I woke up when you went outside. At first, I thought you'd gone to the outhouse alone but I couldn't believe you'd be so stupid. This isn't a game out here, Sarah. Sometimes you don't get a second chance."

"I know that," she snapped. "Don't call me stupid. I made a mistake."

"So did I," he muttered as he tended to her cold feet.

"Really? And what mistake was that?"

"I brought you here. I should have left you on the side of the road. I don't need to be responsible for another person, for the decisions you make. It's not my fault if you do something that'll get you killed."

"What do you want me to say?" Sarah demanded.

He stood up. "I don't want you to say anything. Just stay here. I'm going to get more wood for the fire. Don't move."

"I won't," Sarah assured him. She watched him leave, stunned by his reaction. Sam had always seemed so laid-back, the kind of guy who never let his temper get the best of him. But she'd seen fear in his eyes and wasn't sure where it had come from. Yes, she'd made a mistake, but everything was all right and she was safe now. Left to her own devices, surely she would have found the cabin again.

Sarah rubbed her arms. Was his anger really about

her? she wondered. Or was Sam just mad because he felt anything at all? When he walked back inside the cabin, he barely acknowledged her, his expression as cold and dark as the storm raging outside.

"I don't think you're angry at me," she murmured.

"Don't be so sure," he muttered, dropping the logs next to the hearth.

"No. I think you were scared. Scared I might get hurt like your friend, Jeff."

Sparks showered onto the hearth as he tossed a log on the embers. "Don't try to psychoanalyze me." He stood and turned to her, regarding her with a cool indifference. "You're wet. Take off those sweatpants and get back into bed."

Bristling at his tone, Sarah opened her mouth, ready to jump into an argument. After all, what right did he have to punish her for a tragedy in his past? But she saw the warning in his eyes and decided to retreat.

She didn't want to experience the worst of Sam's temper right now, especially when there was no way she could storm out and slam the door behind her. Grudgingly, she acquiesced, crawling out of the rocking chair and pushing the pants down over her hips.

Sam pointed to the bed. "Crawl in." After grabbing the down sleeping bag, he followed her and once she'd snuggled beneath the blankets, he threw the sleeping bag on top of her.

Sarah shivered, tucking her hands between her legs. "It's really snowing out there," she said in a feeble attempt to make conversation.

"It's a spring storm. It'll last a few days and then the snow will melt and everything will be fine."

Somehow, she sensed that he was talking about the storm inside the cabin. "I'm sorry," she murmured.

When the fire was crackling, Sam returned to the bed. He kicked off his boots and socks then stripped off the rest of his clothes. When he was dressed only his boxers, he tossed back the sleeping bag and blankets and crawled in beside her.

"You're cold," she murmured. She moved away from him, afraid that touching him might make him angrier.

"Give me a few minutes, I'll warm up."

Sarah wasn't sure what to do with her hands. But then, Sam slipped his arm around her waist and pulled her against his body. She snuggled up against him and rubbed her cold feet up and down his legs. She felt secure again. As long as his arms were around her, everything would be all right. Gradually, their body's heated the blankets and the chill began to dissipate.

"I wasn't afraid," she said. "Not really."

"You should have been."

"I knew you'd come and get me."

Sam pulled her even closer. Sarah's breath stilled and she tried to relax, to forget about where she was. Here, in his arms, she felt completely safe. She could trust Sam with her life. He would have risked his own life to save hers and that realization was too much to wrap her brain around.

But then, she felt the same way. If he'd been caught in the storm, she would have gone out to find him, without a thought for her own safety. What did that mean?

She wanted to turn in his arms and kiss him, to

make up for the mistake she'd made. In the end, she counted backward from one hundred. And when she still wasn't asleep, she began again. And when sleep finally came, her dreams were plagued with fleeting caresses and soft sighs and the tantalizing touch of a man she couldn't see.

6

SAM WOKE to the feel of Sarah's hands on his body. At first he thought he was dreaming, but as he slipped the bonds of sleep, the sensations coursing through his body became very real.

Her hand smoothed along his belly, then gently skimmed over his hard shaft, the fabric of his boxers creating a tantalizing friction. "What are you doing?" he asked, his voice still ragged with sleep.

He felt her breath warm on his chest and her hair tickled his chin. "If you don't know then you've been out in the woods far too long."

"Sarah, don't," Sam warned.

She slid her hand up the leg of his boxers and wrapped her fingers around his erection. He bit back a groan, his resistance dissolving in a heartbeat. He knew what this was about. She wanted to set things right between them and she was using sex to do it.

She'd been right about his outburst last night. He hadn't been angry at her, just frightened and then relieved. Feelings he'd once controlled so carefully had turned on him. Sarah Cantrell was a desirable, sexy woman. But now she was *his* desirable, sexy woman.

He'd begun to see what it would be like to have her in his life. Though he'd never been in love before, his feelings for Sarah were coming dangerously close to an emotion that he'd conscientiously avoided.

Her fingers circled his erection and the breath slowly left his body. Maybe it was still just about lust, about the uncanny way Sarah had of making him want her. "I thought we weren't going to do this," he said in a strangled whisper.

"That was a bad plan," she replied. "I've had reason to reconsider."

"And what reason might that be?"

"I have a nearly naked man in bed with me. I'm not one to let a good opportunity pass me by. Besides, I don't have to worry about mixing business with pleasure anymore. Now, it can be all about pleasure."

Sam sucked in a sharp breath as she began to stroke him, her hand moving in a slow and easy rhythm. He couldn't imagine a better way to wake up. Hell, how many mornings had he opened his eyes and found himself with an aching erection that he couldn't do anything with? This was a fantasy come true.

He arched against her touch and let the pleasure wash over him. The things she could do to him with just a simple caress. Sarah pressed her lips to his chest and then ran her tongue over his skin until she teased at his nipple. When she drew back and blew softly, he shivered, the cold and the anticipation heightening the sensation. His fingers slipped through her hair and Sam tried to pull her back up to kiss him.

But Sarah seemed determined to explore new territory with her mouth and tongue. And when she disappeared beneath the blankets, Sam knew what was coming. He braced himself for the shock and a few seconds later, her tongue met the tip of his shaft.

His breath caught and he held back a moan. Her lips were soft and warm as she took him into her mouth. How could something so simple cause such a violent reaction? His heart slammed in his chest and he gasped for breath. He wanted to jump out of his skin every time she drew away, certain he'd explode if she continued.

Sam closed his eyes and tipped his head back, trying to focus his mind on something other than the exquisite feel of her tongue. He was so close, just a heartbeat away, but he couldn't allow himself to come.

He braced himself on his elbows and threw back the covers. "I want to be inside you," he murmured. The sight of her taking him into his mouth again sent another shock wave coursing through his body.

"We can't," Sarah whispered.

"We can," he countered.

She shook her head, her hair brushing against his belly. "We don't have any condoms."

Sam groaned then flopped back into the pillows. "And you don't have any?"

"Sorry," Sarah said. "You could always run out to the corner drugstore." She smiled drily. "Or maybe we should figure out what the pioneers did...or I could just carry on."

He knew all the arguments against unprotected sex, but for the first time in his life, desire was outweighing common sense. That's how badly he wanted to lose himself inside her, to feel that sweet warmth of her body around him.

And then, she drew him in again and it was suddenly no longer an issue. He watched her seduce him with her mouth, her hair tumbled around her face, her lips teasing and tormenting him until he was afraid to breathe, afraid to move.

Sam tried to last as long as he could, to enjoy every moment of ecstasy she offered. And when he was finally there, he surrendered quickly, the intensity of his orgasm shattering his control. Her fingers finished the job that her mouth had begun. As she coaxed the last bit of his desire from him, Sam felt a curious peace settle over him.

How could he ever live without this? Or more importantly, how could he live without her? In such a very short time, she'd made a place for herself in his life and now he couldn't imagine this cabin without her in it.

Sarah brushed her hair out of her eyes. "Good morning," she said.

"I'm glad I didn't leave you out in that snowbank," he said, raking his hands through her hair.

"And I'm glad you're not still mad at me." Sarah crawled out of bed and crossed to the fireplace, then tossed a few logs on the fire. Sam's gaze skimmed up her long slender legs and came to rest on her sweet backside.

"When I woke up this morning, I was listening to the wind outside," Sarah said, "and I was thinking that this was like a fantasy I used to have as a kid."

Sam rolled onto his side and braced his hand beneath his head. "You had fantasies like this when you were a kid?"

She hurried back to the bed and crawled beneath the covers. Sam pulled her body against his, tucking her head beneath his chin.

"It wasn't a sexual fantasy. Have you ever seen

that movie *Swiss Family Robinson?*" she asked. "It's about a family who gets shipwrecked on a deserted island and they make a whole life for themselves out of things they find on the island. When I was little, I was determined to find a way to live my life on a deserted island. I'd swim in the ocean and build a house in the trees and have a baby elephant for a pet. Until now, I forgot all about that fantasy. But this is like living on an island. We're cut off from the world, dependent on our own resources."

"Maybe that's why you were so determined to make this television program," he said.

She smiled. "Maybe. But I don't think it was the wilderness element that attracted me as a kid. I think I saw a perfect family in that movie and I wanted it for my own. They were on this island, all alone, and they only had each other. No one else could come along and ruin things." Sarah laughed softly. "So now that I've told you a deep dark secret about myself, you have to return the favor. Tell me something that no one else knows about you."

Sam considered her request, searching his mind for something she might find interesting. "I once ran the New York Marathon without ever training for it. I was in bed for nearly a week after that."

"That's not a very good secret," she said.

"All right. When I was eight years old, I decided to take my father's car for a drive. It rolled down the driveway and smashed into the neighbor's car. I never confessed to the crime and he spent the next few months arguing with the dealer, claiming that there was something wrong with the car."

"Not bad," she said. "But you can do better. Dig deep."

Sam took her hands between his, warming her fingers. She had such soft, delicate hands. He toyed distractedly with her fingers, then measured his palm against her. "I never cried after my mother died."

A long silence descended over the cabin and Sam risked a glance over at her, surprised that the words had come out of his mouth. It wasn't exactly a secret; he'd just never had cause to say it out loud. "Not once. Not when she was sick and in the hospital, and not at the funeral. She was my mother and I never shed a tear."

Sarah reached up and cupped his cheek in her palm. "She knew you loved her. Your tears wouldn't have been for her, they would have been for you. For what you'd lost. Mothers know those things and they understand."

He'd carried the guilt around in his heart for so long, ashamed that he hadn't been able to give his mother that much, certain that it meant there was something fundamentally wrong with him. But now, it was as if Sarah had opened a door and let light into all the dark parts of his soul. She'd granted him absolution.

"That was a good secret," she said. "It felt good to say it, didn't it?"

Sam drew her toward him and kissed her. "Now you. Tell me a secret no one knows."

She snuggled closer, nuzzling her face into his chest. "When I was ten, I found out that my father was having an affair with his secretary, if that isn't the biggest cliché. One night, I snuck out, took her garden hose and put it through her mail slot and turned on the water. I didn't realize that she had gone out of town for the weekend with my father on a business trip. When she came home, her house was flooded and all the floors and carpets were ruined. There was a front-page article about the vandalism in the *Belfort Bugle*. But no one ever suspected it was me."

"How long did the affair last?" Sam asked.

Sarah shrugged. "I don't know. It didn't really matter because there was another after that, and then another and another. And my mother just turned a blind eye. I remember one day I came home from school and I found her on the kitchen floor. She'd taken some over-the-counter sleeping pills. Not enough to kill her, but enough to scare me. I never told anyone about that. It was our little secret."

"We're a pair," Sam murmured. "Full of secrets." He slowly stroked her hair.

"I've never wanted to tell anyone before. It's difficult for me to trust people," Sarah admitted. "Especially men. But I trust you."

"I'll never lie to you again, Sarah."

She pushed up on her elbow and pressed a lazy kiss to his shoulder. "I understand why you came here," she said. "But don't you ever think about leaving?"

"I do leave. All the time. I spend days in Sutter Gap during the summer, picking up supplies, and... other necessities."

"Picking up women?" Sarah teased.

"Occasionally," he admitted. "Does that bother you?"

"No, not at all. It's only natural that you'd have... needs."

"But when I finally come up here for good in the fall, I'm usually happy to be alone. That wears off toward the end of February, though. And then, until the snow melts, I have a very active fantasy life."

"What kind of fantasies?" Sarah asked, her expression curious.

Sam chuckled. "Just the typical guy stuff."

"And what's the typical guy stuff?"

"Why are we talking about this?" he asked.

"Come on. Tell me all your secrets." She paused. "On second thought, let me guess. Threesome?"

"No," Sam said.

"Sex in a public place?"

He shook his head.

"I know. Bondage."

"This morning," he said, catching her gaze and holding it. "Waking up with you in my bed. Having you...touch me the way you did. That was my fantasy."

Her smile faded slightly. She scrambled off the bed and walked over to the fireplace. "What should we have for breakfast? If we're going to hike back down the mountain, I want to have a good breakfast."

Sam stared at her for a long moment, wondering about her sudden shift in mood. She'd gone from intimate to playful to aloof in a matter of minutes. "I don't think we'll be going down today," he said.

She spun around. "Why not?"

"Open the door."

Sarah crossed the room and pulled on the door. A huge drift had packed against the rough planks and it tumbled inside. She jumped back, but the snow covered her bare toes. "There are at least two feet of snow out there!" she exclaimed, slamming the door shut.

He nodded. "Spring storms can be pretty bad. It would be dangerous to start down in the middle of one. The footing is treacherous and the hike would be exhausting. It'll melt in a few days. We'll go down then."

Sarah's shoulders slumped. "I can't stay. I have to get home."

Sam tossed back the covers and crawled out of bed. "You don't have any choice," he said. "There's nothing we can do but wait for the sun to come out and melt the snow."

"So what are we going to do all day?" she asked.

Sam had a few suggestions. But considering they didn't have the proper supplies—namely condoms—he might be forced to suggest more mundane activities. "There are plenty of things to do. You'll see."

SARAH STARED at the chessboard. She knew she was beat. Sam had given her every chance to win, but she'd managed to maneuver herself into check and there was no escape. "I hate this game," she muttered.

"That's because you don't think before you move," Sam explained.

She eyed him, wondering if he was referring to her little trip to the woodpile earlier that morning. "If I took as long as you to make up my mind, we'd be here all day."

"That's the point," Sam said. "We have plenty of time, so why rush?"

"Isn't the objective to finish the game? To find out who wins?" She stood up and began to pace the cabin. "I don't know how you stand this. With two of us here, at least there's conversation. But what do you do when you're alone?"

Sam glanced down at the chessboard. "Sometimes I play with myself."

Sarah turned and looked at him, then burst into laughter. It was apparent Sam didn't see the humor in his statement. But then realization dawned and he rolled his eyes.

"Chess," he explained. "I play chess with myself."

Sarah continued to giggle, so uncontrollably, that her eyes began to fill with tears. It felt good to laugh. Things between her and Sam had gotten far too serious. After their conversation that morning, she felt as if they'd revealed too much. They'd only known each other for a few days and yet they'd told each other their deepest secrets.

"Are you going to include that in your program?" he taunted. "Sexual self-gratification in the wilderness. You could do at least a few hours."

"Is that how long it takes?" she asked.

"When a guy has all day, he doesn't need to hurry."

"There is no sex on PBS," she said. "Don't you know that?"

Sam grabbed a rook and threw it at her, but she dodged it. She ran around to the other side of the table and grabbed a handful of pieces off the board. An instant later, they were hurling chess pieces at each other in a heated battle, ducking behind the table and scrambling to pick up ammunition from the plank floor.

When he'd gained an advantage, he lunged at her and pinned her to the floor. Sarah wriggled to free herself, arching her back and twisting against his grip.

But Sam easily pinned her arms above her head. He leaned forward, as if he meant to kiss her and she suddenly stilled, her gaze fixed on his mouth in anticipation.

He bent closer and her lips parted. "You want to kiss me, don't you?" she said breathlessly.

"Nope." Sam playfully licked the tip of her nose.

"Ewww!" Sarah cried.

He licked her cheek and then her chin.

"Stop!"

"Not until you give up," he said.

"All right, I give."

He let go of her and she scrambled to her feet, wiping at her face with her fingertips. "That is just disgusting."

Sam slowly stood, his hair falling in his eyes. Sarah resisted the temptation to smooth her fingers through it. Every time she touched him, she wanted more.

"So what do you want to do?" Sam asked. "We could play cards or checkers."

"I can't do what I really want to do," Sarah said.

"And what is that?"

"Right now, I would love a long, hot bath. With bubbles and candlelight. And scented shampoo for my hair. And a big fluffy towel to dry myself with. That would be pure heaven."

"You really want a bath?"

"You don't have indoor plumbing. So I suppose you're going to tell me to go find a river and jump in."

Sam shook his head. "I can get you a hot bath."

"How?"

He cocked his head. "If I get you a bath, what will you do for me?"

Her eyebrow rose as she considered her answer. "I'll...make dinner. And do the dishes."

"Not good enough," Sam said.

"I'll fetch the firewood."

"No, I don't think that will do it."

Sarah paused, then reached out and toyed with a button on the front of his flannel shirt. She leaned into him and turned her face up, smiling playfully. "If you get me a hot bath, I'll let you watch."

Sam grinned. "Deal."

"Deal," she repeated.

Sam grabbed his jacket and hurried outside. A few moments later, he returned with a huge washtub. He dropped it on the floor in front of the fireplace. "I carried a lot of supplies up this mountain, but this was the worst. Carter offered to bring it up on his ATV, but I said no. Now, I'm kind of glad I went to all the effort."

"That's the bathtub? I'm not going to be able to sit in that."

"You don't take a bath sitting down. You do it standing up. You wash your hair first, then do the rest of your body and then rinse."

Over the next hour, Sam heated water in a big pot outside then hauled it into the house in a pair of buckets. When the tub was full, he grabbed a towel and a fresh bar of soap from the dry sink, holding it out to her.

"No shampoo. But the bar soap works well. I'll go get a little more water for your hair."

Sarah unbuttoned the flannel shirt she wore and let it drop to the floor, then knelt next to the tub. She sniffed the soap and recognized the simple scent of Ivory. "I guess this is better than nothing," she murmured as she stuck her head in the water.

Though it was easy to get her hair wet, it was almost impossible to work up lather with the bar of soap. Sam stepped inside with the buckets and she turned to look at him. "I can't do this," she said. "It doesn't work."

He shrugged out of his jacket and then knelt beside her. "Here. Give me the soap and then sit down on the floor with your back against the tub."

Sarah did as she was told. "Now what?"

"Now just tip your head back." He poured a bit of the water from the bucket onto her hair, then began to work the soap through it. "It just takes a little more effort."

"What do *you* do when you want a bath?"

"Well," Sam said. "When I want to feel all pretty and pampered, I bring in the washtub. But usually I walk down to the creek, get naked and soap up."

"In the winter?"

"Yeah, on the warmer winter days, I will. It's a bit chilly, but it's a hell of a lot quicker than heating all that water. If it's bitter cold, I just wash up at the dry sink."

Sarah closed her eyes as Sam worked the lather through her hair. He gently massaged her scalp, sending tiny frissons of pleasure coursing through her body. "This is heaven," she murmured.

Sam picked up one of the buckets and rinsed her hair, then wrapped it in a towel. "All done," he murmured.

When she opened her eyes, she found him staring at her face, his hooded gaze skimming lazily over her features. He stood, then held out his hand to help her up. Sarah sighed. Right how, he could strip off all her clothes, carry her to the bed and make love to her, and she'd be perfectly content. They'd grown so close and she wanted to feel that connection physically as well as emotionally.

Sam turned her around to face the bed and an instant later, unhooked her bra. "What are you doing?" she asked.

"Getting you naked. Can't take a bath with your clothes on, can you?"

"No," Sarah said. "Sure can't." She stood quietly as he finished undressing her, his hands moving over her in a slow, sensual caress. With each item of clothing he removed, he took the time to smooth his palms over her skin, sending tingles of anticipation up and down her spine.

He knew her body so well already, as if he'd memorized every curve and angle, every inch of naked flesh. Sarah had never wanted a man to know her that intimately, but she loved that Sam did. They're shared the secrets of their pasts and the secrets of their bodies. And yet she wanted more.

"You make me happy," Sarah said.

He took her hand and helped her into the tub, then let his palm slide over her hip. His gaze caught hers and they stared at each other for a long moment. It was a simple statement, but it came from deep inside her heart.

"Then I guess I'm doing something right," he said. He dropped a quick kiss on her mouth, then grabbed a sea sponge from the table. He soaked it with warm water and drew it over her body, wetting every inch of her skin.

Sarah felt so exposed, so vulnerable, standing in front of him, completely naked. She contemplated taking the sponge from him and bathing on her own, but letting him work at the task was like tantalizing foreplay, sending desire spinning through her body.

"That feels so good," she murmured as he washed her back. He moved up to her shoulders and Sarah slowly turned and wrapped her arms around his neck. "Maybe you should share my bath. It's a shame to waste all this hot water."

Sam chuckled softly. "Don't you think that would be tempting fate?"

"No. I just think it would be tempting." She reached for his shirt and unbuttoned it, then slid it down over his shoulders. When he offered no resistance, Sarah continued, taking the time to appreciate each and every part of his body as she exposed it.

She knew the small mole on his neck and the soft trail of hair beneath his belly button. She knew the scar on his elbow and the Chinese symbol tattooed on his back below his shoulder. "What does this mean?" she asked, running her fingers over the dark ink.

"Inner peace," he said. "Serenity."

"That's nice." She pressed her lips to the spot, then smoothed her hands over his back. He truly was a beautifully made man, lean, yet muscular, long-limbed and perfectly proportioned. When she slid his boxers over his hips, his desire was already evident. Sarah reached out and ran her fingers along the length of his shaft, but her gaze was fixed on his.

She saw it in his eyes, the undisguised need. His hands skimmed over her shoulders, his fingers just barely meeting her skin. "Do you know what you do to me?" he murmured. "I don't know who I am anymore."

She drew him into the tub and fished the sponge out of the water, then slowly began to wash his body.

She dragged the sponge over the sharp angle of his collarbone, down the rippled muscles of his abs, and around his finely muscled buttocks. Sam braced his arms on her shoulders as she gently worked around his erection, the soapy water dripping down his thighs.

Every touch became a prelude, every soapy caress an offer of the pleasure that their bodies might share. Sarah wanted him desperately, the feel of his skin against hers, the warmth and the weight of his body as he moved inside her. The reward outweighed all the risks. "Make love to me," she murmured, pressing her mouth to his chest.

"I can't," Sam said. He let his hand drift down to the damp juncture between her legs.

"We can," she urged. "There's nothing stopping us. Just think of how wonderful it will feel. Absolutely nothing between us. It'll be perfect."

"We don't have to do that to make it perfect," he said. "Touching you, having you touch me, that's perfect, too." Sam nuzzled her neck. "Touch me, Sarah."

She wrapped her soapy fingers around his shaft and gently began to stroke him. At the same time, he found the sweet spot between her legs. Sarah gave herself over to his caress, her pulse quickening and her breath coming in short gasps.

At first, complete surrender had been almost frightening for her. But now, it felt exhilarating and liberating. Her body belonged to him and nothing could hurt her. This wasn't just sex anymore, it had become an act of faith.

As he carried her toward her release, Sarah brought him along. Every movement seemed new and exciting, the two of them learning the language of each other's needs. Each sigh, each soft moan and whispered plea sent them closer, their desire piqued by the simplest of acts.

Sarah danced on the edge, the nerves in her body trembling with anticipation. Sam whispered her name, begging her to slow down, but she wanted to feel him come before she lost herself in her own release. He cried out once, his knees buckling slightly, then gave himself over to his orgasm. A moment later, Sarah joined him, falling against him as spasms rocked her body.

As the pleasure subsided, Sarah knew what they'd shared had been so much more intense than intercourse. They'd allowed themselves to know each other's bodies as they'd known their own.

Sam nuzzled her neck and sighed deeply, his breath slowly returning to normal. Then he reached down and grabbed the last bucket of hot water, pouring it over them both. "I told you it would be perfect," he murmured.

Sarah gave him a satisfied smile. "Perfect," she murmured.

THE SNOW STOPPED falling by the second afternoon and though they'd spent the entire previous day in bed, Sarah was still restless. Sam watched as she poked at the fire, running a stick back and forth through the embers.

Though he couldn't think of anything more stimulating than another afternoon in bed, they were dancing dangerously close to the edge. No condoms meant a limit to what they could share. And it was getting harder and harder to keep from leaping across that line.

It was also getting more difficult to accept that, very soon, Sarah would no longer be with him. Once the snow melted, he'd take her back to Sutter Gap and she'd return to her own life. Maybe it was time for him to start reminding himself of that reality, to maintain a bit more distance and perspective.

Yet he couldn't bring himself to draw away. He felt as if he were rolling down a mountainside, gathering speed. The trip was wild and thrilling, yet there was always the chance that he'd fly off a cliff or run into a tree. But right now, Sam didn't care. Every minute he spent with Sarah was real and true. How could he deny himself?

He walked to the door and picked up his pair of Wellies. "Come on," he said. "We're going outside."

Sarah glanced over her shoulder. "It's too snowy. My feet will freeze."

He held up the Wellies. "You can put these on over your shoes."

The prospect of getting out of the cabin caused her spirits to lift almost immediately. She grinned and Sam felt a rush of warmth pump through his bloodstream. It was so easy to make her happy. After all they'd experienced together, he was still moved by her smile.

"What are we going to do?" she asked.

Sam grabbed his jacket. "Let's take a walk. I've got some snowshoes we can strap on. We'll go exploring. As long as you're here, you might as well learn something about the woods."

She stopped. "If we can go exploring, why can't we walk back to Sutter Gap?"

It was a good question. In truth, they probably could walk back. Although it would be a hard slog through snow drifts, it wouldn't be impossible. But after a few hours, Sam was certain they'd both be exhausted and would be forced to make camp. Until the cold broke and the snow melted, it was just easier to stay put. Besides, he wasn't ready to let her go just yet.

"We're not going far," he said.

Sarah shrugged and put on her shoes, then struggled to pull the boots over them. When they were on, she stood, her eyes bright with excitement. "Not bad."

Sam handed her a warm jacket, then dug out a cap and a pair of leather gloves from the crate near the door. When she was bundled against the cold, he put on his own jacket and retrieved the snowshoes from the corner near the fireplace.

They stepped outside into a pristine wonderland. The heavy snow clung to the trees, tiny branches bending under the weight. Sarah drew a deep breath of the clean air and closed her eyes, tipping her face up to the sky. "I'm beginning to love this place."

Sam was struck by how truly pretty she was. Even without a bit of makeup, her face was undeniably beautiful, especially when she smiled.

A crack split the silent air and she jumped. "What was that? It sounded like a gun."

He bent to strap the snowshoes onto her boots, Sarah holding on to his shoulder for balance. "The snow is so heavy it breaks limbs off the trees. They've been snapping all night." He finished with the last strap then sat back on his heels. "Take deliberate steps, don't try to hurry. The snowshoes will distribute your weight, so you won't sink down into the snow, you'll walk on top of it."

He watched as she ventured away from the cabin, testing herself with the clumsy footwear. After a few strolls back and forth in front of him, she shrugged. "It's not that difficult."

But as she turned to walk away from him, she caught one edge of her snowshoe beneath the other and began to list to one side. A moment later, she tumbled into the snow. Sam hurried over and pulled her to her feet, brushing the snow off her backside. "It's not that difficult," he teased, mimicking her voice.

"If I start to roll down the mountainside, promise you'll catch me," Sarah said, dusting off her legs.

Sam chuckled and strapped his snowshoes on, then pointed to the east. "I cut a little path through the woods last summer. It should be a fairly easy walk."

The snow crunched beneath their feet and as they brushed against the trees, the branches vibrated, showering soft, fluffy snow over them both. Sam had never seen a more gorgeous day, made even more so by the woman with him.

Though he knew they were great together in bed, it was nice to find they could do something outside the house as well. She was his lover, but that wasn't where it ended.

When they'd gone a hundred yards down the trail, Sam stopped and pointed to a tree. "That's a chestnut tree," he said.

Sarah craned her neck to look up at it then nodded. "That's nice."

"In a winter survival situation, it provides food. Nuts are the best source of energy you'll find. In the summer, the woods are full of things to eat, but in the winter, you look for nut trees." He dug around in the snow and pulled out at chestnut. "Throw this in the fire and roast it. Or if you have a way to boil them, they'll get soft and you can mash them, like potatoes."

Sarah nodded and took the chestnut from his hand, then slipped it in her pocket.

They walked a bit farther and Sam pointed to another tree. "Black walnut. They're all over these woods and they're very nutritious."

He indicated a wild filbert tree and then walked toward a small stand of pines. "In the spring, you can collect the young cones from pine trees and boil or bake them. They make an excellent meal. Plus, you can use the resin for glue—or even for a temporary dental filling."

Sarah examined the pine cones at the end of a bough and then frowned.

"What are you thinking?" he asked.

"I was thinking how good you would have been on the show." She turned and walked back to the path, Sam staring after her. He'd been thinking the same thing—not about how good he might be, but how good they'd be together. Making Sarah's program would be a way to keep her in his life for a lot longer than the next few days, maybe long enough to figure out how he really felt about her.

But was he ready for that kind of commitment, to turn his life upside down for a one in a million shot at something? Not at fame or fortune, but at love. Real and deep and lasting love.

Over the past three years, he'd never once thought about love, about finding a woman who'd become part of his life and part of his future. But now, the idea teased at his mind almost constantly and he found himself seriously considering the notion.

"I think I might be able to survive out here if I had to," Sarah said.

"You know how to make fire and find food. What about water and shelter?"

"Well, I'd find a stream or a river. And boil for twenty minutes."

"In the winter, it's better to melt snow. You don't have to boil it and in a survival situation, you might not have anything to boil it in. In summer, there's rain water and dew."

"At least I know how to make a shelter," Sarah said.

"And how is that?"

"Well, first I find a big long stick and rest one end up on a rock or a stump or the crook of a tree, not too far off the ground. Then I make a tent with a lot of other sticks and I throw leaves and branches on top of it. Then I crawl inside as snug as a bug."

"A debris hut," Sam said. "Where did you learn that?"

"I read your article. You built one when you first came up here, just to see if you could survive in such a basic shelter. That story was what got me interested in doing the show."

Sam stared down into her face, her cheeks pink from the cold and her warm breath clouding in front of her face. It had become so easy to touch her, almost second nature to him now. Kissing her was like breathing, absolutely necessary to sustain life and so instinctual it didn't take any thought at all. If he leaned forward now, his lips would meet hers and his blood would instantly warm.

She reached for him as if to draw him closer, but Sam grabbed her hand. "Come on, we're almost there."

As they hiked, the trees began to thin and a few minutes later, they stepped into a wide meadow. Sarah stopped, shielding her eyes from the sun with her hand. "Is this the cabin you told me about?" she asked.

Sam nodded. "This was probably all cleared by hand, maybe to plant a crop or a garden. Some of the logs were used for the cabin."

It was like a tiny oasis in the middle of a thick forest. In the summer, it was the only place to catch the sun for most of the day. "On a warm day, I'll hike over here and just sit," he said.

They walked through the meadow to the ruined cabin. The door rested at a crooked angle, its hand-wrought-iron hinges rusted through and the roof had long ago rotted and caved in. He pulled the door and stepped inside, then reached back for Sarah's hand.

"How old do you think it is?" she asked, walking over to the fireplace that dominated one end of the room.

"There's no telling. This area was settled well before the Civil War so maybe 1840 or 1850."

She ran her hand along a rough-hewn timber that served as a mantel then paused. "Look at this," she said. Sarah quickly snatched off her glove and ran her fingertips over a spot in the wood, straining to see. "There's something carved here."

Sam stepped to her side. "It looks like initials. D.E.R."

"And A.C.R.," Sarah added. "I'll bet that's who lived here," she said, a faintly dreamy look on her face. "David or Daniel. And Alice, or maybe Ann." She smiled softly and stepped back.

"If you were Alice, would you have followed your David into the wilderness?" Sam asked.

Somehow, he sensed that this was the most important question he could ask her, not whether she wanted him or needed him, or even if she was falling in love with him. He needed to know just how far she'd go to be with him.

Would she give up everything she knew for him? He forced a smile, then turned away from the mantel. What difference did it make anyway? He wasn't David and she wasn't Alice and they lived in the twenty-first century, not in 1840. Choices were a lot easier in the modern world.

Sarah continued to stare at the carving. "I can't understand it," she murmured. "What would ever possess a woman to come out here and live in the middle of nowhere?"

"A sense of adventure?"

"Don't you think that's more of a male quality? Come on, honey, pack up the kids and the furniture. We're heading west." She joined him near the door. "To come out here and be so completely vulnerable to the elements, to luck and to fate. People got sick and they died. When they came west, they left families behind, relatives they'd never see again. And Alice would have had to raise her children in these woods, all alone, without a doctor nearby."

"Maybe Alice loved David. Maybe she couldn't imagine life without him."

"I don't think I could have done it," Sarah said. "I'm not that brave."

"It doesn't take bravery," he said. "Everyone is scared sometimes."

"What does it take then?" she asked.

He considered the question for a long moment. "An act of faith? A complete belief in the person you're with, that between the two of you, you can solve any problem."

Sarah glanced over at him, her brow furrowed in confusion. "I'd still be scared," she said.

Somehow, Sam sensed that they weren't talking about David and Alice anymore. When they'd begun, that night in the Lucky Penny, they'd had so many obstacles standing between them. Over the past few days, those had all gradually fallen away. Now there were possibilities here that hadn't existed before.

He took her hand and kissed the spot above the top of her glove. "We should probably get back."

As they walked through the meadow toward the path, Sam stared to the east. Last summer he'd found two headstones buried under some brush. They were nothing more than large rocks that had been rolled to the spot and then crudely carved. The largest rock had Alice's initials and the smaller, the initials of what Sam assumed had been a child.

It was a sad ending to their love story, yet a stark reality of their existence. Living in the wilderness, so far from civilization, a man had as much to lose as he had to gain.

7

SAM STARED at the ceiling above the bed. The sun was already up and he knew the snow was melting just by the warmer temperature inside the cabin. In addition, a steady drip sounded just outside the front door and birds that had flown for shelter in the midst of the snowstorm were now singing brightly.

Sarah was nestled in beside him, her naked body curled against his, her arm thrown over his belly. He'd prepared for bed last night with every intention of maintaining a proper distance, but Sarah had entertained other ideas. She'd peeled off all her clothes in a playful striptease, then started in on his, tempting him as he'd reluctantly surrendered each item of clothing.

In the end, Sam had given up the fight, making love to her with his hands and his mouth. What use was it anyway? After their discussion at the old cabin, he knew exactly where she stood. Sarah had no illusions about living in the wilderness. When the time came, she'd happily walk off his mountain and back to her old life without a second thought.

But he also knew how he felt. So he'd enjoy the time they had left, without any hesitation or guilt. He'd take what she offered and consider himself lucky.

Sam sighed, throwing his arm over his eyes. But was he really lucky? Letting her go would cut deep and the wound would take time to heal. Had he been more aware, he might not have allowed himself to get so attached. But somewhere between their first night together and this very moment, he'd surrendered his heart. He wanted Sarah Cantrell, maybe even loved her. But how much was he willing to give up to have her?

She stirred beside him and Sam shifted, willing away the erection that had greeted him upon waking. Her touch had a powerful effect on his body, but merely having her lie beside him was enough to tease his body into readiness. Hell, all she really had to do was look at him and he'd get hard.

Sex with Sarah had turned into a tantalizing mix of desire and denial. Though they couldn't completely surrender to their bodies' demands, they'd discovered a connection that was deep and stirring and strong. And yet, at other moments, Sam felt as if the connection was so tenuous it could be broken with just one wrong move or careless words.

Wincing, he pulled his arm out from beneath her head and rolled off the bed. He grabbed his jeans from the floor and tugged them on, shrugged into a shirt, then walked over to the door. When he pulled it open, a fresh breeze blew in. Sam closed his eyes and drew in a deep breath. "Tomorrow," he said. "One more day and all this is over."

He pulled on a clean pair of socks and his hiking boots, then grabbed the axe and slipped out the door, not bothering to button his shirt. The chilly air hit his bare chest, erasing the haze of sleep and desire. He walked around the side of the cabin to the woodpile.

A stack of unsplit logs sat on the end of the pile and he tossed a few near an old stump.

Balancing one on its end, he swung the axe and split the wood. One by one, he worked through the small pile, then stacked the split logs against the cabin. Before long, a sheen of sweat covered his chest and he barely noticed the chilly weather.

After about a half hour of hard work, he heard the front door of the cabin open. Sarah, bundled up in his jacket, handed him a cup of coffee then sat down on the stump. "I didn't hear you get up."

Sam waved the axe in the direction of the woodpile. "I thought I'd get some work done. We can't stay in bed forever."

She stared up at the sky. "It's warmer. The snow is melting."

He didn't have to ask what she meant by her words. The subtext was clear. It was time to leave his mountainside and take her back to her life. "We can probably head back tomorrow. The snow will be melted by then if this weather holds."

Sarah stood and wiped her hands on her jacket. "So what should I do to get ready?"

"You could help me finish splitting this wood. Grab one of those logs off the end of the pile and set it on the stump."

She did as she was told and Sam rested the axe on the end of the log and split it. They worked together for a long time, methodically moving through the pile of wood, the axe the only sound to keep them company. When Sam stopped to take a break, she grabbed the axe from his hand.

"You want to try it?" he asked.

"Sure."

Sam grinned and took the axe back. It had taken him nearly six months to perfect the art of splitting wood. She'd barely be able to lift the axe, much less split a log. "All right. Watch carefully. You want to stand with your legs slightly apart so you get good balance. Then put the axe right where you want to hit the log. Then just swing it around and—"

The axe cracked through the log, the two pieces falling away on either side of the stump. "Now, you try," he said.

Sarah took the axe from him. "I know it's not that easy. If it were, there would be a lot more lady lumberjacks."

Sam laughed. She looked so silly, in his oversized coat and Wellies, her nose runny from the cold. "It's not that hard. It isn't about strength, it's about accuracy."

As she rested the axe on her shoulder, Sam placed another log on the stump. She slowly lowered the axe and took aim. But when Sarah swung the axe around, she missed the stump entirely and hit the ground in front of her foot.

He caught her before she tumbled into the snow. "Geez," Sam cried. "Be careful. I don't want you chopping off your foot."

"Maybe you should show me how to do it again," she said.

"I think we better leave the wood-chopping to more experienced hands."

"No, I want to see you do it again," Sarah insisted, her chin tilted up at a challenging angle.

Sam repositioned the wood on the stump and took an easy swing. But the moment the wood split, Sarah grabbed a handful of snow and shoved it down the back of his shirt.

With a low growl, he dropped the axe and spun around. Sarah screamed and ran, stumbling through the snow in the oversized Wellies. He aimed a snowball at her and it exploded against the back of her head. She headed for cover behind the trunk of a large tree.

Laughing, Sam gathered up another handful of snow and waited. When she didn't appear, he ran toward the tree, ready to dodge any incoming snowballs. But just before he reached her, his foot slipped out from under him. As he began to fall, he tried to catch himself. But his ankle twisted beneath him and Sam heard the distinctive snap of a breaking bone.

He landed with a soft thud, sharp arms of pain ripping through his leg. He moaned and when he tried to move his leg, the pain was excruciating. Sarah peeked around the tree. "Are you playing dead now?"

He cursed softly, then brought his arm up to cover his eyes. She approached slowly, as if she thought he was playing some kind of trick to lure her out of hiding. When she got close enough, she hurled a snowball at him, but he did nothing to counter the assault.

"Are you giving up?" she asked.

"I think I'm going to have to." Sam winced as he braced his hands behind him and sat up, the snow clinging to his clothes and stinging his bare skin. "I think I may have just broken my ankle." He paused. "No, I don't think. I know."

"Don't kid around," Sarah said. "That's not funny." But the moment she looked into his eyes, she realized he wasn't joking. She knelt down beside him. "Are you sure? Maybe it's just sprained."

"I felt it crack. Right above my ankle. I broke my

leg skiing when I was a kid. I know what it feels like."

"What should I do?"

"Help me up."

Sarah offered him her hand and he struggled to his feet, pitching forward into her arms. A string of vivid curses slipped from his mouth at the pain. Sarah caught him before he fell again and he wrapped his arm around her shoulders. Slowly, he hopped to the cabin, the pain so intense he felt nauseous.

Once inside, Sam moved to the table and sat down on one of the stools, gingerly propping his leg up on another one. But he couldn't get comfortable. Every tiny movement was enough to send another round of pain racing through him.

"Now what?" she asked.

He shrugged. "I don't know. I'm just glad you're here. If this had happened when I was alone, I would have been in big trouble. I couldn't have chopped wood, which means I wouldn't have been able to stay warm. And fetching water would have been difficult."

"What are we going to do?"

"We need to put a splint on it to stabilize the bone. That should help with the pain. See if you can find some sturdy sticks out near the woodpile. Not too big around. But before you go, give me one of the towels. And there're scissors under the dry sink."

Sarah nodded, the fear evident in her expression. When she left the cabin, Sam used the opportunity to remove his boot and examine his ankle. Sam knew it was a nasty break, probably both bones, right below the top of his boot.

Though he could curse his clumsiness, he'd have to deal with the problems it had caused. There was no way he could walk down the mountain for help. He couldn't even crawl without unbearable pain.

When Sarah returned to the cabin, she was carrying an armload of sticks. "I wasn't sure what you wanted. If they're not right, I'll look for more."

Sam nodded, then pointed to the towel and scissors. "Cut some long strips."

Her hands shook as she picked up the scissors and Sam reached over and took them from her. He pressed his lips to her palm, then held her fingers in his. "It'll be all right. Don't be afraid."

"What are we going to do? I—I know I keep asking you that, but I don't have any answers. I hope you do."

"Nothing," Sam said. "There's nothing we can do but wait."

"I could go for help," Sarah said.

He laughed softly. "You don't know how to get back to Sutter Gap on your own. You got lost going to the woodpile, remember?"

"It was night, it was snowing and I couldn't see. That doesn't mean I can't find my way down this mountain. You could draw me a map. I can follow directions."

"No," Sam said, shaking his head.

"We can't just stay here, Sam. If you don't get medical treatment for your ankle, it may not heal properly. This is serious."

"A few more days won't make a difference. Besides, sooner or later someone will come for you. Someone will notice that you've been gone too long, they'll track you to Sutter Gap and Carter Wilbury will walk up here and see what's going on. Once he comes, everything will be fine."

"And what if he doesn't come for two or three weeks?" Sarah asked.

"Someone will check up on you before then. A friend or a co-worker will get curious."

"Maybe not," she said. "Libby Marbury is the only person who knows where I am. And she knows I was hiking up the mountain to find Sam Morgan and that my cell phone doesn't—" Sarah's words died in her throat. "My cell phone! I brought my cell phone along."

She raced to the door and grabbed her jacket, then found her phone zipped in an inside pocket. She flipped it open, but when she powered it up, there was no signal.

"It won't work," Sam said. "Unless you get to higher ground, you won't get a signal. Even then, the reception can be spotty."

"Where is higher ground?" Sarah asked.

"I'm not going to let you go," Sam insisted. "It's too risky. You don't know your bearings out there, Sarah."

"But you can teach me," she said.

"Like this? If I can't walk, how can I teach you to survive in the wilderness? Sarah, people have hiked into the woods and never been seen again. This isn't some city park with paved paths. If you get lost, you might never find your way out." He winced as he shifted on the stool. "The first thing we need to do is splint my ankle. And I have to find a way to keep it elevated and to ice it."

Sarah nodded. "All right," she said. "I need to find something waterproof. The water bag, should work. I'll fill it with snow. And we can rig up a sling above the bed."

How long could he wait? Sam wondered. Sarah was right, help might not come quickly. And he wasn't a doctor, he didn't know the consequences of leaving the break untreated. But pioneers must have broken arms and legs all the time and survived. The bones would set themselves over time.

Hell, he had no intention of sending her off on her own. The risk was just too high. She could get hurt or lost or even worse. And he'd never be able to live with that. She meant too much to him.

Sam grabbed a pair of sticks and steeled himself for the pain that would come with splinting his ankle. If he just didn't show any concern, maybe he'd be able to convince her to wait. If not, there wasn't much he could do to stop her.

SARAH NESTLED into the warmth of Sam's body, taking care not to jostle his leg. She'd rigged up a sling of sorts that elevated his ankle and provided stability while he slept. But she wasn't sure it was doing any good. If his leg wasn't set properly, there was no telling what might happen.

It had been two days since Sam had broken his ankle and in that time, she'd gone through a storm of emotions. At first, she'd been terrified, unable to cope with her fears. She imagined all the worst things that could happen—the break could cause a blood clot and he could die. His foot could turn gangrenous and he could die. He could try to walk down the mountain, fall off a cliff and he could die.

The only thing she was able to learn from her fears was that she didn't want to lose him. In just a week,

Sam had become a part of her life. She'd never wanted it to happen, but she supposed it must have been a done deal before she'd even realized how far it had gone. Over the past two days, watching this man she so cared about deal with his injury, she'd felt trapped, caught between her concern for him and her doubts about herself.

But then the fear had worn off, and Sarah had known what she had to do. Sam needed her help. There was no one else. So she'd insisted that he teach her everything she needed to know about wilderness survival. He'd thought he was simply appeasing her, finding a way to occupy her mind while they waited for help to arrive. But she'd decided she'd have to force the issue.

She'd hike up to higher ground and take the chance there would be a cell phone signal. And if she couldn't get one, she'd come right back to the cabin and they'd make alternate plans. Sarah carefully crawled out of bed and sat down on the floor. Sam's clothes were stored in crates beneath the bed. She pulled the crates out and began to search for brightly colored clothing.

She found a yellow parka and an orange vest. After grabbing them both, she spread them on the table, then picked up the scissors and began to cut the nylon fabric.

"What are you doing?"

Sam's voice startled her and she glanced up from her work. "Bread crumbs," she said.

"What?"

"I'm making myself some bread crumbs. Like that old fairy tale. I'm cutting these jackets into strips and I'm going to tie the strips to the trees so if I need to, I can use them to find my way back."

"Find your way back from where?"

"I'm going to climb up to the ridge today and see if I can get a cell phone signal. Don't bother arguing, because you won't change my mind. We've waited two days and your ankle looks worse. I'm not going to sit around here any longer while you're in pain."

Sam sighed, then laid back against the pillows. "I thought we discussed this, Sarah. I can wait."

"We did discuss this. And I know your objections, but I'm still going. Now, you can either draw me a map or you can let me wander around out there on my own. It's up to you."

"My ankle feels a lot better," Sam insisted.

Sarah stared at the splint, shaking her head. "The swelling still hasn't gone down and you're in more pain than you're willing to admit. Don't lie to me. You promised you'd never lie to me again."

He pressed his lips into a tight line and nodded. "It will get better," he said.

Sarah knelt on the floor beside the bed, crossing her arms on the edge of the corn-husk mattress. Sam turned and rested his arm on her shoulder, toying with her hair as she spoke. "We have to do *something*," she murmured.

He drew her closer, touching his lips to hers, his tongue running along the crease of her mouth. But this time Sarah pulled away. Sex had been a simple distraction he'd used to divert her attention, but it wasn't going to work anymore. "Stop worrying and come back to bed," he murmured.

"No! And you stop acting like this is no big deal!" Sarah cried. "You *are* lucky I'm here. And since I am, I'm going to help."

"You could help by taking off all your clothes,"

Sam said. "That would make me feel a lot better, I swear."

"That's not funny," Sarah said, pushing away from the bed.

"No, it's not. I was dead serious."

"Well, I'm not going to let you use my body as a convenient painkiller." Sarah grabbed his backpack from where it rested on the end of the bed. "I'll need a compass if you have one. And a couple of flashlights in case I get caught out in the dark. I'll take the tent, and the sleeping bag if you can do without it." She glanced over at Sam and saw the frustration in his expression. "Don't even think about yelling because it won't help."

With a low curse, Sam struggled to sit, then slipped his ankle out of the sling. He swung his legs over the edge of the bed, wincing as he moved. Sarah watched him stand, then hop over to the kitchen table. If he planned to physically keep her from leaving, she knew he'd fail. She was much quicker on her feet than he was and if she had to kick him in the foot to make her point, she would. Whatever additional damage that caused could be fixed by the doctors.

"All right," Sam said, nodding to himself. "But you're not leaving here until I'm convinced you know what to do out there."

Sarah crossed the room. Wrapping her arms around his neck, she drew him close. All she needed was the assurance that he believed in her. Beyond that, she could do whatever was necessary.

Over the next hour, Sam grilled her on every aspect of survival. When she didn't answer correctly, he'd go off on a rant, his temper conveying his worry. But then, he'd calm down and continue, making certain that she understood every risk and problem she might encounter.

As they talked, Sarah set up and broke down the tent, reviewed her understanding of the compass and listened to Sam's warnings about bears. She also packed the supplies she'd need, taking care to plan for at least one night out in the wild. And to make sure she had a fire, Sam gave her matches and a lighter.

Though the walk should take about three hours, Sam was determined to cover any contingency, short of her falling down the mountain and breaking her neck. He scribbled out a detailed map and then added two extra pages to show her where she shouldn't go. Between the map and her bread crumbs, she was certain to find the way.

While he finished, Sarah opened the front door. The day was warm and sunny and the snow was nearly gone. Though the path would be slippery and muddy, Sarah now had Sam's boots to protect her feet. With warm, dry feet, she could walk all day.

"I'm ready," she murmured.

Sam glanced up from his map-making, staring at her for a long moment. "You're sure?"

"I'm not changing my mind now."

He held out his hand and she moved to the bed to take it, squatting beside him. He pulled her into his embrace. "Don't make me regret this, Sarah. If anything happens to you, I'll never forgive myself."

"Nothing will happen," she said, smiling. But even as the words came out of her mouth, she knew what was running through his mind. All of the fears that he'd confessed to her were back in full force. He already blamed himself for his friend's death. He didn't want to put her life in danger as well. "It's just a walk in the park."

Sam drew back, then cupped her face in his hands and kissed her deeply. "Carter Wilbury told me you were a powerful-stubborn woman. He didn't know the half of it."

Sarah smiled, running her fingers through his hair. "When we get back to Sutter Gap you're going to have to set him straight."

"Go," he murmured, his lips skimming over hers. "Before I try to stop you again."

Sarah nodded, then turned and walked to the door. She grabbed the pack and hoisted it over her shoulders, then gave him one last smile before she stepped outside. As she closed the door, she drew a deep breath and gathered the tattered bits of her courage.

"You can do this," she murmured. But as she walked, fear began to creep in, not for her own safety, but for Sam's. What if she got frightened and couldn't go on? What would happen to him then? Or what if she did fall off the mountainside and kill herself? Who would help him then?

She continued to walk, putting one foot in front of the other, glancing down at the compass to guide her. The footing was tricky, but even with the pack on her back, she felt strong and energized. Perhaps it was the adrenaline pumping through her, bolstering her courage.

When she'd gone a fair distance, Sarah stopped and turned around, hoping to take one last look at the cabin. But it had been swallowed up by the woods, the structure blending in to the grays and browns of the surrounding landscape.

As she climbed higher, she kept her eyes on the ridge above. But her thoughts constantly returned to the cabin, to the man she'd left there. And suddenly, Sarah knew, deep in her heart, that she would do anything to help him. The revelation was like a slap to the face, jolting the last bits of fear from her mind.

This was what it was like to love someone, she mused. To be willing to sacrifice anything and everything for that person. "Oh, God, do I love him?" Sarah shook her head. "Of course not. I care about him, that's all."

She looked up, searching for the spot where the ridge was cut into a deep step. At first, she didn't see it, her gaze skimming back and forth along the line between the earth and the sky. But then Sarah found it, sighing with relief. All the landmarks were exactly where they were supposed to be.

Minutes turned to hours, but Sarah continued to walk, ignoring the exhaustion cramping her legs. The pack felt like dead weight on her back and she knew she could move much faster if she just left it behind. But she knew that dropping the pack would mean a greater risk. "I'll drop it at the top of the ridge," Sarah murmured.

Instead of thinking about her aching back and her tired legs, Sarah focused her thoughts on Sam. She hadn't always been so cynical about love. When she was younger and a bit more naive, she'd thought maybe there was a man out there for her, a man who valued fidelity over fun and games. As boyfriends came and went, Sarah realized that every man had imperfections. After a time, those imperfections began to grate until they became intolerable.

She hadn't yet figured out Sam Morgan's flaws.

Sarah had begun to wonder if he had any at all. Sure, he was a little bossy. And overprotective. And he lived in a cabin in the middle of the woods. But none of that made any difference to her. It didn't change the man he was, the man she'd come to depend upon.

"I don't need him," Sarah murmured. Once she got back to Belfort and slipped into her regular routine, everything would sort itself out. She was just so used to his company now that it was difficult to imagine a day without him. But they hadn't been living in the real world. Instead, they were living in her childhood fantasy, cast away on a deserted island with no choice but to be together.

As Sarah picked up her pace, she made a promise to herself. She wouldn't regret anything she and Sam had shared, not from their first night in bed together to her decision to walk away.

When she reached the notch in the ridge, Sarah slipped her arms out of the pack and set it against a tree. She had a short climb to the highest spot, ten more minutes at the most. She turned and looked back down the mountain, stunned at how quickly she'd made it to the top. But when she looked at her watch, Sarah realized that it had taken her over three hours to make the trek.

She grabbed her phone from the pack and flipped it open, then said a little prayer before she switched it on. "This will work," Sarah murmured as she put the phone to her ear. A dial tone crackled and Sarah sighed in relief. Then a whoop of joy burst from deep inside her and she did a little happy dance.

If she climbed just a bit higher, the signal might be better. As she scrambled up the last rise, she allowed herself to envision what would happen after she made the call. She'd hike back down and tell Sam the good news, then wait with him for help to arrive. But with that thought, the impact of her actions began to set in. The satisfying sense of accomplishment she felt became tempered with a stark reminder of what she was about to lose.

By tomorrow, they'd be back in Sutter Gap and after that, they'd go their separate ways. And over time, her memories of Sam Morgan would fade, as had the memories of all the other men in her life.

Still, it would take a long time for her to forget, as it would take a long time to convince herself that she could live without him.

SAM STOOD in the front door of his cabin, staring out into the woods. He'd spent the morning counting the minutes and then the hours, watching the sun cross the sky and trying to imagine where Sarah was. Though his injured ankle made pacing difficult, it hadn't stopped him. He'd hobbled outside and found a stick, then managed to fashion a crutch from it.

By now, Sarah should have reached the ridge line and discovered whether her cell phone worked. The hike back down would be quicker than the hike up, but the landmarks weren't as visible so there was a greater risk she'd get lost.

He'd calculated her time of arrival and when it had come and gone, he'd recalculated and continued to hobble back and forth inside the cabin. She was already an hour later than he'd expected. Sam drew a deep breath in an attempt to calm his nerves. Hell, *he'd* even missed the cabin on some of his hikes. How was she supposed to find it?

He'd experienced fear like this before, that day on the mountain with Jeff. But there, he'd at least been able to respond, despite that it had been in vain. He felt powerless now, waiting for Sarah and wondering if she was safe, second-guessing his decision to let her go.

But it hadn't really been his decision, he reminded himself. She'd made the choice. With a soft curse, Sam turned away from the door, hopping toward the bed. He tested his foot along the way, trying to put weight on the splint, but the pain was still debilitating, stealing the breath from his lungs. Even if he wanted to go out and search for her, he'd have to do it on his hands and knees.

Sam thought back to that day on the road, when he'd found her sitting on her suitcase. He should have sent her away right then. But he'd been so caught up in his attraction to her that he hadn't been able to think clearly. Would this be another mistake he'd come to regret?

Sam sat down at the table and stared at the chessboard, the pieces frozen in the middle of a game they'd played the previous afternoon. He cursed then rubbed his eyes with his hands.

He'd been so careful not to let this happen again. His mind flashed back to the day he'd come face-to-face with Jeff's parents. He knew they hadn't blamed him. Yet he'd wished that he'd been the one to die that day. With no family left to mourn him, his death would have barely been noticed. Jeff had parents and sisters and brothers and a whole town that had come to his funeral.

Would he have to face Sarah's parents and tell them horrible news? Hell, he didn't even know where to find them if he had to. She lived in a place called Belfort and she had a friend named Libby. Beyond that, he knew virtually nothing about her, yet she was putting her own life in danger to help him.

She must care about him a great deal, Sam mused. He moved the chess pieces around in an attempt to occupy his mind. But he couldn't sit still. He limped back to the door and flung it open. Putting his fingers in his mouth, he whistled as loud as he could then shouted her name.

His voice echoed in the woods and he listened, praying he'd hear a reply. And then he did. But it wasn't Sarah's voice.

"Sam Morgan!"

Sam waited and a few minutes later, Carter Wilbury appeared at the bottom of the trail. "Carter! Damn, am I glad to see you." He watched from the doorway as his friend climbed the last few yards to the cabin. Carter carried a backpack that he dropped on the ground when he reached Sam.

"I hear you had a little accident," Carter said with a wide grin. He bent down and examined Sam's foot.

A wave of relief washed over Sam. "You talked to Sarah?"

He shook his head. "Nope. I talked to a friend of hers. Some lady named Libby from South Carolina. Miz Cantrell called her and this lady called the Lucky Penny. As luck would have it, I was sittin' right at the end of the bar."

"She's all right then?"

"I guess. The lady said Miz Cantrell was on her way back down the mountain after she had a short rest and some lunch."

"How did you get up here so quickly?"

"Brought my ATV. I trailered it up to the head of that old logging road on the back side of the west ridge. Then I drove it in from there. Only took me two hours. It was a quick trip, but I had to leave it down below once I hit the steep section. Boy, that thing is a whole lotta—"

"Did you see her?" Sam asked.

"Who?"

"Sarah. She hiked up in that direction to call for help. I sent her up to the notch on the ridge."

Carter shook his head. "Nope, didn't see her. Though I 'spect she'll be coming along shortly. Now, we need to get you down. There's an ambulance waiting on the highway. I can't guarantee that it'll be a smooth ride, but they gave me some pills that might make you feel better."

"I'm not leaving," Sam said, shaking his head. "Not until Sarah gets back."

Carter scowled. "That ambulance isn't gonna wait. You need to go now. Listen, some of the boys are coming up the trail on their ATVs. We'll leave Miz Cantrell a note and have her wait here. I'll come back and bring her down."

"What if she's lost?" Sam asked. "By the time you get back here, it'll be dark."

"Then I'll send Dub Watley and the boys from the Lucky Penny out to find her. They've been itching to tear up my mountain. Now, get your jacket on. We've got a fair walk before you can ride."

Every instinct in Sam's body told him to wait. But he couldn't do anything to find her. Turning the boys from the Lucky Penny loose on the mountain was the best way to make sure she was safe. And he trusted

Carter more than he trusted himself when it came to wilderness search and rescue.

But he also had to trust Sarah. She was prepared to spend the night outside if she had to. She knew how to make a fire and cook a meal. She had his tent and his sleeping bag. Sam closed his eyes. Of course she'd be fine.

"All right. I'll go down with you. But you and the boys have to promise you'll find her and bring her right back to Sutter Gap."

"I know this mountain like the back of my hand," Carter assured him. "I'll find her. And if she's too tired to go back down this evening, we'll stay here tonight and come back early tomorrow. Now, why don't you write her a note? I've got some stuff in my pack to make you a little more comfortable."

Sam scribbled a few lines on a pad of paper, then tore it off the pad and crumpled it up. There were so many things he needed to tell, feelings he wanted to express. But trying to compose his thoughts in a rush was impossible. He just had to trust that he'd see her again and that he'd have a chance to say all the things he wanted.

He wrote a few quick words and when he was finished, Carter helped him get ready. He pulled a removable cast from his backpack and helped Sam fit his foot inside it, then tightened the Velcro straps.

Sam stood and was surprised at how much better his ankle felt. It was completely immobilized and he could move with only minor pain. Though he still couldn't put weight on his leg, with Carter's help and his wooden crutch, he could get around a bit easier.

Sam took a last look around the cabin before Carter closed the door behind him. As they stumbled down the narrow path together, Sam tried to convince himself he was doing the right thing. And as the cabin faded from view, he promised himself if Sarah wasn't safe by the next day, he'd crawl up the mountain, cast and all, to find her.

8

SARAH PULLED the car off I-40 at the Biltmore Avenue exit in Asheville. She snatched up her map from the passenger seat and squinted at the hand-written directions to Mission Hospital.

The past few days had been a test of her nerves, her will and her courage. But she'd surprised herself, pushing aside her fears and doing what had to be done.

By the time she'd hiked back down to Sam's cabin, he'd already gone. She'd found his note and waited for Carter to return, relieved that help had finally arrived. When he did return, the older man explained that Sam had been taken by ambulance to Asheville. Sarah had insisted that they start down the mountain immediately, but Carter and his friends from the Lucky Penny had convinced her to rest for the night and leave the next morning. So she'd spent the night, and much of the next morning, in Sam's cabin with six snoring men.

Sarah glanced at the clock on the dashboard. Visiting hours at the hospital probably ended at eight. It was nearly six. Though she'd been assured Sam was fine, Sarah wasn't going to believe it until she saw for herself.

The hospital parking lot was brightly lit and she

pulled into a spot near the front entrance and parked her car. The attendant at the information desk looked up as she approached, welcoming her with a smile.

"I'm looking for Sam Morgan's room," Sarah said.

The woman scrolled down a computer screen then nodded. "Room 347. Ride the elevators up to three and then take a right. It's near the end of the hall."

Sarah smiled. "Thanks."

As she rode the elevator up, she nervously toyed with a button on her jacket. It seemed so odd to be back in the real world, in the midst of a busy city, with the traffic and the noise. Her time alone with Sam had been a welcome vacation that she suddenly longed to return to.

It felt as if they'd lived a lifetime on that mountain. She and Sam had shared an experience that had brought them closer than any two strangers should have ever come. And now that they were away from the cabin, she knew everything would be very different. She was actually nervous about seeing him again, wondering if he'd be the same man she'd come to know.

Sarah had considered writing him a letter, saying her goodbyes without another face-to-face meeting. After all their talk about no-strings sex and one-night stands, there really was no reason to prolong their farewells. But she also knew there was something more between them, something left unsaid. If she just saw Sam once more, maybe she'd know what it was.

The elevator doors opened on three and Sarah stepped out then hurried down the hall. She found Sam's room and rapped softly on the door. When he didn't answer, she pushed the door open and stepped inside.

She found him lying in his hospital bed, dressed in a standard issue gown, a sheet draped over his hips. His right leg rested in a sling that was held up by ropes and pulleys. The television played softly in the background, illuminating the nearly dark room.

She reached for the light switch beside the door but thought better of it, choosing instead to watch him for a few seconds longer. Sarah slowly approached the bed. He looked so different. Dressed in something other than denim and flannel, she barely recognized him.

Sarah held her breath, taking in his profile now cast in light and shadow. She'd grown so accustomed to seeing him every day. Already, she'd missed the sight of his handsome face, his boyish grin and his intense blue eyes.

"Hey there," she said softly. "Are you awake?"

Sam turned, and when he saw her, he smiled sleepily. "Hi. I was wondering when I'd see you again."

"Here I am," Sarah said.

"God, you look good. Just as beautiful as I remembered."

"And look at you," Sarah said, suddenly uneasy with the compliment. "Nice cast."

He knocked on the plaster that began beneath his knee and covered his foot. "The traction is just to keep my leg elevated. They operated on my ankle yesterday evening. Put in a plate and some screws to hold the bone together, but it should be good as new in a few months. I've already been up and around on crutches, so it's not so bad."

"Does it hurt?" Sarah asked.

"Nah. They've been giving me these nice little pills. I could fall out of bed and not feel any pain."

Sam reached out and Sarah hesitantly wove her fingers through his. She was almost afraid to touch him again, certain that once she did, she'd never be able to stop. It felt so good to have that reassuring contact.

With a soft sigh, he pressed his lips to the back of her hand. "I'm glad you're all right," he said. "I was worried."

"I did fine. Going up was difficult and then when I came down, I accidentally took a little detour. I ended up at the old cabin. But once I got there, I knew where I was. And then I found your note and I knew you were going to be all right." She wove her fingers through his. "I told you everything would be fine."

"I didn't want you to leave," Sam said. "Did the boys take good care of you?"

"They were perfect gentlemen. But don't be surprised to find your cabin a mess when you get back. They brought along a lot of beer. And they decided to cook breakfast this morning and it was a disaster."

Sam gave her hand a squeeze and she fought the urge to cover his face with kisses, to let her tightly held emotions loose and crawl right into bed with him. They'd been apart for only a day and a half, but Sarah had missed him so much that she ached inside.

"You're a very determined woman, Sarah Cantrell."

She laughed softly. "I was pretty scared out there all by myself. But I remembered what you taught me and I tried to stay calm. I knew if I got in trouble, I could handle it. I could build a shelter and make a fire and find water."

"If I had been alone up there, there's no telling how long it would have been before help arrived. I'm not sure I could have crawled down that mountain."

He stared into her eyes and she could see the need there. He wanted to kiss her and touch her and assure himself that everything was still good between them. All it would take was just one kiss and this uneasiness would disappear.

But then Sam looked away, fixing his gaze on the television set.

Sarah glanced around the hospital room. It felt as if a barrier stood between them now. "How's the food here?" she asked, scrambling for a safe topic of conversation.

"Not great." He pointed to his unfinished dinner on the tray.

"I should have stopped and picked up a burger for you."

"You've already done so much," Sam said. "You don't need to take care of me anymore."

"You needed my help," Sarah said. "You would have done the same for me."

A long silence descended over the room as Sam continued to play with her fingers. "Sometimes I think we've known each other for years," he finally said. "And then I remember we met just over a week ago."

"I was just thinking the same thing."

"You put your life at risk for me and I barely know anything about you. I don't know about your family, I don't know what kind of car you drive or where you live or what you like to eat for breakfast. All I know of you is what we shared in the cabin. And somehow, that doesn't seem to be enough now."

"Wasn't that the way it was supposed to be?" Sarah asked.

"But it doesn't seem right, does it?"

Sarah's stomach fluttered at his words. Did he want her to stay? Was that what he was asking? Sarah stared at their fingers, so tangled together she couldn't tell which were his and which were hers. She'd had that problem lately, trying to remember where she left off and he began. They weren't a real couple, but they felt like one. "I'm going home tomorrow," she said brightly.

"To Belfort," he said.

Sarah nodded.

"And you'll see your family?"

"My mother is probably wondering where I've been."

"And your father?"

"I guess he'll be happy to see me, too." Sarah frowned. He was in such an odd mood. She wondered if he were suffering from the lingering effects of anesthesia. Or maybe the painkillers were messing with his mind. Or perhaps he'd realized, as she had, that they'd come to the end of their time together and he was trying to make things easier for her.

"So you're headed back home," he repeated. "That's good."

Why had conversation become so excruciatingly difficult? "Tomorrow morning. I thought I'd get a room here in Asheville tonight. There's a motel just down the road." She stood up and walked to the window, then fixed her gaze on the parking lot below. "I—I'd love to stick around, but I've got to get back to work. Now that *Wilderness* is off my schedule, I'm left with *Billy Bob Barkley's Bass Fishing Bonanza*. First thing I'm going to do is shorten that title." She turned back to him. "What are you going to do when you get out of here?"

"Carter has an extra room at his place, so I'll probably recover there. But I thought I might do a little traveling once I'm up and moving around, maybe head up to New Hampshire to visit Jeff's family and see some friends in New York. I don't believe I'll be hiking up any mountains until this cast comes off." He cleared his throat nervously. "I've been thinking about your idea for the show. Maybe we ought to do it."

Sarah blinked in surprise. "You don't want to do the show, Sam. I know you don't. Besides, I don't think it's a good idea anymore. You took me up that mountain so that I'd understand and now I do. That place really isn't about adventure or survival. It's about healing. What you're doing is personal and private and it shouldn't be exploited...even if I would exploit it in a very tasteful manner," she added with what she hoped was a smile.

"But if we did the show, we'd see each other every now and then, wouldn't we?"

Sarah gathered her resolve. Though it would be easy to believe in the fantasy, she couldn't allow herself even a daydream. "I thought you were looking for a no-strings arrangement, remember? And I think it would be best if we kept it that way. We're just at two different places in our lives right now."

Sarah groaned inwardly. It all sounded so predictable. She'd used those words so many times before with men far less worthy than Sam Morgan. He didn't deserve trite platitudes and feeble excuses. He deserved the truth. Leaving him would be the most difficult thing she'd ever done in her life. Her heart felt as if it were being ripped from her chest and she still wasn't sure she could actually follow through. But she had to try.

"That doesn't mean I won't miss you," he said. "I've gotten used to having you around."

"Just don't go breaking any more limbs," Sarah warned, trying to lighten the mood. "I'm not going to be there to rescue you." She bent closer to place a gentle kiss on his cheek. At the last moment, he turned and their lips met for one sweet moment.

"It's been fun," he said when finally she drew away. "No regrets."

"No regrets," Sarah said, smiling at him. With that, she let go of his hand and walked to the door, desperate to make her escape while she still could. Then she turned back to him, needing to see him just once more. "Bye, Sam."

"See ya, Sarah."

When she reached the hallway, Sarah stopped and leaned up against the wall. For once, she wasn't going to second-guess herself. The past week had been a wonderful respite from her real life, a time to learn just a little bit more about the woman she was. Though Sam's world on his mountain was in some ways very real, in others it was an illusion, where life, and love, seemed much simpler than they actually were. The passion they'd experienced in that little cabin could never flourish anywhere else.

"Catch and release," she murmured. This time she'd throw the man back before the relationship had turned all tired and depressing and confusing, before she'd fallen out of love with being in love. Sarah closed her eyes and smiled.

Sam was the best fish she'd ever caught and the only one she'd ever considered keeping. That had to count for something, right?

"I HAVEN'T WATCHED television for nearly a year and there still isn't anything on," Sam muttered.

The night nurse held out a tiny cup containing his pain medication, but he brushed it aside. "It will help you sleep," she insisted.

"I don't want to sleep." He continued to flip through the channels on the hospital television, searching for anything that might distract him. But he knew only one thing could possibly satisfy him now and she had walked out of his room a half hour ago.

"The Braves are playing on channel seven," the nurse said. "Are you a baseball fan?" She gave him a smile as she smoothed the bedcovers with her hands. Sam glanced over at her.

Under any other circumstances, he would have jumped right in. She was quite pretty, her blond hair pulled back into a tidy knot at the nape of her neck, her willowy body almost hidden by a set of shapeless scrubs. She'd already stopped by his room twice since Sarah had left and he'd gotten the distinct impression she was flirting with him.

Sam shifted on the bed, his body stiff from lying in the same position for an entire day. He wasn't used to spending hours flat on his back—except for the time he'd spent in bed with Sarah and he had no complaints there. But those times were behind him now. Sarah was gone and he had to move on, the quicker the better.

He ran his hands through his disheveled hair then returned her smile. "I'm not much of a Braves fan. But I used to follow the Yankees." He paused. "Do you like baseball?" He glanced over at her name tag. "Nurse Franklin?"

"Amy," she corrected.

"Amy," he repeated. Maybe a little flirtation was exactly what he needed to take his mind off Sarah. Since she'd left, he'd rewound their conversation over and over again in his head, searching for some clue to her feelings. But the more he thought about her, the more frustrated he became.

It was obvious that things were over between them. But he couldn't ignore the desire he'd seen in her eyes when he'd touched her hand or when she'd kissed him. As much as she tried to hide it, she still wanted him.

"I do like baseball," Nurse Amy said. She picked up his chart and scanned it. "On a scale of one to ten, can you tell me your level of pain?"

"It was about a three or four," Sam said, "until you walked into the room. Now I hardly notice it."

She laughed softly then made a notation on the chart. "So, I noticed your wife didn't stay very long. That was your wife, wasn't it?"

Sam shook his head. "No, I'm not married."

Her expression brightened considerably. "Your girlfriend then?"

"No," he said. But then Sam stopped and considered her question. "Yes. No." He cursed softly. "Yes," he repeated. "I guess she is my girlfriend." A slow smile spread across his face.

Suddenly, he didn't want to spend his evening flirting with Nurse Amy. He didn't want to spend his evening with anyone but Sarah. And if he could walk up and down the halls on his crutches, he could certainly get himself out of this damn hospital.

Nurse Amy frowned, clearly confused. "So you do have a girlfriend?"

"Where are my clothes?" Sam asked, tossing back the bedcovers. "I need my clothes and I need you to call me a cab." He reached up and released the sling that cradled his broken leg. "Hand me those crutches."

"You—you can't leave. You just had surgery yesterday and—"

"And I'm feeling much better and I want to get out of here," Sam said. "Now. Tonight."

He could have been dressed in a matter of minutes, but Nurse Amy refused to give him his clothes. He finally found them in a plastic bag on the closet shelf. When his jeans didn't fit over his cast, Sam demanded scissors, but Nurse Amy had turned uncooperative.

She hurried out the door, determined to call his doctor. By the time she returned, Sam had managed to rip his jeans from ankle to knee and had stuck his cast-covered foot through the hole he'd made. He threw on his flannel shirt, not bothering with the buttons, then grabbed his jacket and hobbled out into the hall on his crutches.

"I'm sure I need to sign something so you all don't get in trouble," he said to Nurse Amy.

"You need to know that you're being discharged against your doctor's orders," the desk nurse said. "We can't be responsible if anything happens."

"I can handle that," he said. He turned to Nurse Amy. "Did you call that cab?"

She clucked her tongue. "I still think you should wait for your—"

Sam held out his hand to stop her protests. "Please. I really wouldn't want to walk."

"I suppose I could call the attendant at the front desk downstairs and have her get a cab for you. But I still don't think you should leave."

Sam grinned. "There's nothing you can do to stop me."

A few minutes later, Nurse Amy handed him a clipboard and Sam scribbled his name on the bottom of the form. By the time he reached the lobby of the hospital, a cab was waiting in the drive out front. He crawled in the back seat, pulling his crutches in behind him, and then paused. He wasn't sure where Sarah was staying, only that the place was nearby. But before he found her, he had to make one stop. "Take me to the nearest drugstore," he told the cabbie.

After visiting the drugstore, Sam and the cabbie stopped at two hotels and a bed-and-breakfast before they found Sarah checked in at the Doubletree out near the interstate.

He charmed a pretty desk clerk into giving him Sarah's room number, but when he arrived at her door, he suddenly realized he had no idea why he'd come. He glanced down at the paper bag he carried, a box of condoms tucked inside. He hadn't come for sex, but he wasn't going to be caught unprepared again.

He shoved the bag into his jacket pocket and thought about what he ought to say. He needed to tell Sarah exactly how he felt. There was no denying that they had some sort of relationship, as unconventional as it was. But where did he stand with her? Did they have a future together?

Sam reached out and rapped on the door, hoping that the proper words would come to him once he saw her face.

Her muffled voice came through the door. "Who is it?"

"It's Sam," he said.

A few seconds later, the door swung open. Sarah stared at him, her green eyes wide with surprise. She wore a pair of pink pajamas covered with silly cartoon cats. Her auburn hair was twisted in a knot on top of her head and tendrils hung down around her face. Sam could honestly say she'd never looked more lovely.

"What are you doing here?" she asked.

Sam opened his mouth to explain but suddenly the words weren't there. He couldn't just demand a recitation of her feelings. He had to offer some of his own first. "I know I said I didn't have any regrets. But after you left, I did have one."

He reached out, balancing on his crutches, and put his arms around her waist, intending to pull her into his arms and kiss her. But his right crutch slipped out from beneath his arm. Sam wobbled slightly then felt himself falling forward. He tried to grab the crutch but Sarah caught it instead.

With a tiny scream, she saved him from falling, stumbling backward into the room with him holding tightly to her. They both lost their balance after three or four steps, Sam's cast acting like a weight dragging them both down. In a flurry of limbs and crutches, Sam and Sarah tumbled onto the bed.

Sam lay on top of her, staring down into her eyes.

Her breath came in quick gasps and she stared up at him, unsure of what to do next.

"Are you all right?" she asked.

"If you wanted to get me back into bed," he murmured, "all you had to do was say so."

She arched her eyebrow, regarding him warily. Then with a laugh, she wrapped her arms around his neck and kissed him. In an instant, all the uncertainty between them fell away and they were back to where they belonged—in each other's arms.

Sam growled softly as her tongue teased at his. "I had to see you again," he said. He took her face between his hands and kissed her deeply, desperately. "I couldn't sleep knowing you were so close."

"Are you sure you should be here?" Sarah asked.

"Absolutely," he murmured against her mouth. "I'm right where I belong."

She sighed softly as he drew his tongue along the crease of her lips. "How's your leg?"

"It's broken. It'll still be broken tomorrow, so I'm thinking there wasn't much they were doing for me at that hospital, except feeding me horrible food." Sam kissed her again, this time taking his time, lingering over her mouth until he'd tasted his fill.

Sarah grabbed the collar of his jacket and rolled him over on the bed. Sam winced as the heavy cast twisted beneath her, a sharp pain shooting up his leg. "Careful there."

"Sorry," Sarah whispered. Her knees straddled his hips and she slowly unzipped his jacket. When she found his shirt already unbuttoned, she smoothed her hands over his chest. "So did the doctor give you any restrictions?"

"Are you asking if I can perform my manly duties?"

Sarah pressed her mouth to his chest, nodding.

Her hair tickled his chin. Sam closed his eyes and moaned softly. "I'm pretty sure I'm not broken down there. But maybe we should take things very slowly, just to make sure."

Sarah crawled off of him and stood beside the bed. She reached out and helped him to his feet. Her fingers skimmed over his face, then brushed a lock of hair out of his eyes. With deliberate care, she undressed him, first his jacket and his shirt, then his jeans and finally, his boxers. Her lips found each spot of exposed skin—the inside of his thigh, the small of his back, the nape of his neck. By the time he stood naked, the nerves in his body tingled with anticipation.

His erection brushed against her hip as she moved around his body. Sarah smoothed her palms over his shoulders and then slowly let her fingers drift down over his chest. Sam held his breath, the sensations sending his desire into overdrive.

He fought the urge to unbutton her pajamas and slip them off, to put his hands on her naked body. Instead, he let Sarah set the pace. His own body seemed so in tune with her touch, every caress familiar yet somehow new to him. He'd never grow immune to this, he mused. They could spend a lifetime together and she'd still have the power to drive him wild with just her hands.

Her fingers skimmed along his shaft and Sam sucked in a sharp breath and held it, the heat rushing through his body like a flash fire. He closed his eyes and let the breath slowly leave his lungs. The waiting had turned to exquisite torture, a thrilling mix of pain and pleasure.

"I'm not going to be able to stand much longer," Sam said. His one good leg was getting a little too wobbly to trust.

Sarah gently pushed him back to sit on the edge of the bed. Standing in front of him, she unbuttoned her pajama top, letting the front gape open to reveal a tantalizing view of her breasts. A few moments later, she tugged at the drawstring of her bottoms. They slid low on her hips.

Sam reached out and pulled her toward him. Her body had always fascinated him. It was the perfect complement to his, soft and smooth, all gentle curves instead of hard angles. Sam tugged at the sleeves of her pajamas until the top slipped off her shoulders and fell to the floor behind her. Then he hooked his finger beneath the waistband and tugged the bottoms down to her feet.

Sarah stepped out of them, unfazed by her nakedness. "Now what?" she asked. "I'm all undressed with no place to go."

"We could have a bath," Sam said.

"A bath?"

Sam nodded. Sharing a bath with Sarah was exactly what they both needed. It had worked for them before and it would work for them again.

SARAH STOOD OVER the huge whirlpool tub, hot water pouring out of the brass faucet. When she'd checked into the hotel, she'd asked for a room with all the amenities. After her time in the wilderness, she deserved one night of pampering before she went home. Now she was glad she hadn't opted for the sixty-nine-dollar-a-night motel just down the road.

Leaning over the tub, she ran her hand under the

water to check the temperature. Sarah felt his eyes on her. Glancing over her shoulder, she saw Sam standing in the doorway of the bathroom, dressed in nothing but his cast.

Her gaze raked over his body. He was breathtaking, his lean form honed by hard work, his limbs long and his shoulders broad. They'd grown so comfortable with each other in the cabin that she no longer averted her eyes when he was naked. Now, she just enjoyed the view.

It was odd to see him in this environment, standing amidst the luxuries of marble tile, gleaming porcelain and hot running water. Though the surroundings were different, he was still the man who made her heart pound and her head spin.

"You look so beautiful," he murmured, "sitting there naked, your hair twisted up like that."

Sarah felt a warm flush creep up her cheeks. No man had ever said that to her, at least not that she'd remembered. Yet Sam couldn't seem to stop saying it. Sometimes, he didn't even use words. She'd seen it in the way he looked at her, in the way he touched her body.

When the tub was nearly full, Sarah walked over to him. She noticed a small paper bag in his hand and he gave it to her. "This time I came prepared," he said.

"Do you need help getting in the tub?" she asked.

"I think I can do it. I'm not supposed to get the cast wet though."

Sam sat down on the side of the tub then lowered himself into the water, keeping his right leg on the edge. When he'd settled himself, he sighed deeply and closed his eyes. "Oh, I didn't realize how much

I missed this until now." He opened one eye. "There's room in here for two."

Sarah stepped into the tub and sat down between his legs. She grabbed a washcloth and soaped it up, then gently washed his chest, following the light trail of hair from his collarbone to his belly.

But Sam wasn't interested in the bath, he was interested in what came with the bath. He grabbed her and pulled her on top of him, running his hands down her back until they cupped her buttocks. His lips found hers and he kissed her, their naked bodies sliding against each other as they moved.

The warm water heightened every sensation, making each caress move smoothly to the next. His hard shaft pressed into her belly and Sarah reached between them to stroke it. In response, he murmured her name softly, his breath hot against her ear.

Maybe someday she'd understand what made this all so special with him. Why every sensation seemed to be more intense than the last. Was it the way he touched her or was it the way she responded to him? Making love to him seemed like the most natural thing in the world.

Sam tried to move, but he was trapped beneath her, his leg hitched up on the side of the tub. The water sloshed as he grabbed her thighs and drew them up on either side of his hips. His erection teased at the soft folds between her legs and for an instant, he slid inside of her.

Sarah's breath caught and she shifted so he slipped out. He probed at her entrance, tempting her to simply sink down on top of him. The moment she did, there would be no going back. If she trusted him enough to have no barriers between them, then she had to trust him enough to love him.

His lips found her breast and he drew his tongue around her nipple, teasing it to a hard peak. With every intimacy, they were strengthening a bond between them, drawing closer and closer until Sarah wouldn't be able to think of herself without thinking of Sam as well.

She arched back and took in the details of his face, a face that had become so familiar to her. She knew the tiny scar that marred his left eyebrow and the exact length of his lashes. She knew where to find the dimple on his cheek when he smiled and how his hair curled just beneath his ear.

Sam opened his eyes and found her watching him. They stared at each other for a long moment. And then, as their gazes locked, Sarah let the last inhibition drift away. Slowly, she lowered herself until he was buried deep inside her.

A flicker of surprise passed through his eyes and she froze, wondering if she'd made a mistake, if he might protest. She knew all the risks, but for the first time in her life, she felt not just absolute trust but a desire to give all of herself to someone without holding back. Just once, she wanted this closeness, this perfect vulnerability. And after it was over, she would know what it was truly like to be with a man.

They didn't speak. She just began to move. The warm water in the tub washed up around her hips, sluicing over her skin and surging up his chest. Sam moaned softly, his hands gripping her waist and controlling her tempo.

The feel of him inside her, filling her, touching her so intimately, was enough to send her desire spiraling out of control. She shifted slightly and frissons of pleasure shot through her body. They moved together, joining and then parting, again and again until Sarah could no longer control her need.

Her arms and legs were weightless and her nerves tingled beneath her skin. Sam was close and he measured her pace, burying his face in the curve of her neck. When she refused to slow down, he bit her gently, whispering a warning that was lost amidst her soft moans.

"Tell me you need me," he murmured.

She arched against him, her release just out of reach.

Sam furrowed his hands through her hair at her nape and tugged her head back, forcing her gaze to meet his. "Tell me you need me."

The first wave of her orgasm struck and Sarah cried out. He tightened his grip when she tried to avoid his gaze. A shudder rocked her body. "I—I need you," she admitted. "I'll always need you."

Suddenly, Sam pushed her hips down and held her, but she couldn't stop moving, her climax washing over her in waves. His eyes clouded with desire and he bit his bottom lip. "Don't move."

She ignored his plea and he could do nothing but drive into her, burying himself so deep it ached. His breath caught and then he gasped and joined her in an exquisite release.

The pleasure seemed to last forever, their bodies straining against each other. Then slowly, they tumbled back to reality. When they had both recovered, Sam pulled her body alongside his, his good leg tangled around hers.

Sarah settled in the curve of his arm, her ear

pressed to his chest. His heartbeat thudded against her cheek, gradually slowing. She felt herself drifting with exhaustion that came from complete satisfaction.

Sarah had always wondered how her mother could have spent a lifetime mourning the loss of her husband's love. But now she knew. How would she ever be able to live without this? A tiny shiver skittered down her spine and Sarah shuddered.

Sam drew her closer, his fingers tangling in her damp hair. "Are you cold?" he asked, pressing a kiss to her forehead.

"No," she whispered. He'd always made her feel protected and cared for. She closed her eyes. But how safe could any man really be? She tried to remind herself that the odds of their relationship succeeding were slim at best. For all she knew, Sam could be just like her father, satisfied one moment, then off searching for someone more exciting the next.

But in her heart, Sarah knew that wasn't true. Sam wasn't her father. He cared about her and she trusted him. But was that enough to build a future? Or was she just deluding herself?

"What are we going to do?" Sam asked.

"Sooner or later, we're going to need to get out of this tub," she replied. "We'll shrivel up like a couple of prunes. If you're hungry, we could send for room service."

He caught his finger beneath her chin and raised her gaze to meet his. "I was talking about us, Sarah."

She pressed her face against his chest, avoiding his eyes. She should have realized this was coming. The big talk. Everything had already been decided in his hospital room—a simple goodbye and no regrets.

And then, she'd opened her hotel room door. Now, it was about to turn complicated. "Us?" she asked.

Sam grabbed her hand and wove his fingers through hers, examining her fingernails distractedly. He kissed the tip of her index finger. "Are we really just going to walk away from each other? If that's what you want, then I'm all right with it. But I don't think that's what you want."

"What do you want?" Sarah asked.

He chuckled. "I asked you first."

"I don't know. I've never dated a man for longer than a year. Most last about three or four months. I've always believed in the catch and release approach to relationships."

"And I always insisted on no strings," Sam admitted. "Nothing to tie me down." He bent closer and kissed her gently, lingering over her mouth for a long time before drawing away.

"So how would we ever make it work?" she asked, not really wanting an answer.

"Maybe we're a perfect match," Sam said. "We'd never have any expectations of each other." He kissed the center of her palm.

"I don't think that's very healthy. People in love are supposed to be able to depend on each other."

"Do we love each other?"

"I don't know," Sarah said. "If I did, shouldn't I know?"

"Maybe it isn't about 'should' or 'shouldn't.' I mean, are there really any rules for this?" Sam asked. "Or can we make up our own? This is between you and me, Sarah. It's all new territory for us and we can decide how we want it to work."

She took a ragged breath. "All I know is I don't

want it to get all sad and messy. I can't stand to think that's what might happen. You telling me you need your space and me telling you that I never wanted you in the first place. We had a wonderful time and that's what I want to remember, not some horrible fight six months down the line."

"So once you leave, that's it?"

Sarah hesitated before she spoke. "Maybe we should just go our separate ways and—"

"That's not what I want," Sam said, anger suffusing his voice. "I don't want to believe that I'll never see you again. I can't."

Maybe they'd just accelerate the process and have that fight right now, Sarah mused. Or maybe she could find a way to compromise. "Let's go our separate ways for now and if either one of us wants something more, then we'll find each other again. It's not like we live on different planets, right?"

"So I could come to Belfort?"

Sarah nodded. "Or I could come to your cabin."

He considered her suggestion for a long time. "That's not much of a plan, but I guess it's better than nothing."

Sarah relaxed against him. For now, it was enough. When they said goodbye in the morning, there would be no doubts or uncertainties between them. Instead, there'd be a tiny ray of hope that there could be a future. The real decisions would be left for later.

9

SARAH SAT ON the back porch of Libby Marbury's home, a glass of iced tea in her hand. She'd arrived home the day before and had called Libby to invite her out to lunch, eager to get back to her old life. But she'd arrived at Libby and Trey's house to discover Libby had prepared a lavish welcome-home meal.

They sat on her back verandah, the spring sun warming the old garden, the azaleas in bloom. "You didn't have to go to all this trouble," Sarah said, staring at the array of tasty dishes Libby had laid out on the wicker table.

"I'm finally able to eat during the day without feeling nauseous. The past month, I haven't even been able to face the smell of food before dinnertime. And then after dinner, all I want is my pint of gourmet ice cream."

"You look great, Lib," Sarah said. "Positively glowing."

Libby giggled. "Trey is the one who's glowing. He's so excited, he can barely contain himself. He's already making plans to renovate one of the spare bedrooms into a proper nursery."

Sarah took a sip of her tea. "He just finished the renovations on his house next door."

Libby nodded as she scooped shrimp salad onto

Sarah's plate. "We're going to sell it and put the money in a college fund for the baby."

"It's a fabulous house," Sarah murmured. Her friend's contentment only made Sarah long for the same in her own life. She'd never wanted marriage and a family. But now, she could picture it, and when she did, Sam was in the picture with her.

"After Trey moved in with me, I tried to convince him that you should buy the house next door. We've been best friends for so long and it would be nice to have you close."

"I can't afford that house," Sarah said. "It's just too much to take care of for one person."

"Maybe you won't always be single."

Sarah didn't reply and Libby let the subject drop. But Sarah remembered the discussions they'd had when they were teenagers, talking about their weddings and the men they'd marry. They'd always said they'd live next door to each other and their children would play together and they'd have lunch every day as a loud, happy group.

But sometime after high school, Sarah had decided that a happily ever after with a husband and family wasn't really what she wanted. It was right for Libby but not for her. She never wanted to repeat her mother's mistakes.

But she wasn't her mother. And Sam Morgan certainly wasn't her father. So couldn't she just take the leap, believe that maybe things could work out between them? "This looks just wonderful," Sarah said, turning her attention back to the lunch.

"I have an ulterior motive for my menu choices," Libby explained. "I've been thinking about changing the focus for next season's shows. I know we talked about doing traditional southern dishes, but I'd like to do a series about easy meals for entertaining. Recipes that can be prepared ahead. I've already outlined the new book and I have a whole list of recipes to include and—" Libby paused. "Are you listening to me?"

"Of course," Sarah said, turning back to her. She sent her friend an apologetic smile. "Well, maybe not."

"Would you like to tell me what happened while you were up on that mountain? Because you haven't said anything about it and that's not like you."

"I don't know where to begin. Except to say that…" Sarah took a deep breath. "I think I might have fallen in love."

"Not with that old mountain guy!" Libby said.

"Yes. Sam Morgan. Actually the old mountain guy isn't so old. He's thirty-two, with gorgeous blue eyes and a charming smile and this wonderful strength and competence that made me feel so content and secure."

"You fell in love with Sam Morgan? You were only gone two and a half weeks."

Sarah nodded. "Yes. But that's not the real problem. Like an idiot, I didn't realize how much I loved him until I was driving home yesterday."

"So what are you planning to do about it?" Libby asked.

Sarah picked up her fork and speared a shrimp, then popped it in her mouth. "There's nothing to be done."

"Are you sure?"

Sarah closed her eyes and moaned. "Oh, Libby, this is a great seafood salad. What's the herb you used?"

"You're avoiding the subject."

She'd never been able to fool her best friend. "I can't talk about it. If I talk about it, then I'll start questioning myself. And then, I'll start to believe there might actually be a chance I could have a future with him."

"And why can't you?"

"Marriage has never really been for me," Sarah said.

"Maybe you've never met the right man," Libby said. "Maybe Sam Morgan is him."

"We'll see," Sarah said. "If he is, then I expect I'll see him again. And if he's not, then I'll move on." She gave Libby a desperate look. "Can we please discuss something else? We really should go over plans for next season's shows. Now that I'm not doing the wilderness program, we could get started on *Southern Comfort* right away. We might be able to get our plans done before the baby is born, even tape a few episodes."

Libby laughed. "The camera already adds ten pounds. With all the baby weight, I'll look like the Pillsbury Doughboy behind that counter." She paused. "So how did you leave it with Sam?"

Once Libby grabbed onto a subject of conversation, there was no dragging her away—short of getting up from the table and walking out the front door. "I kissed him goodbye yesterday morning and we went our separate ways. At the time, it seemed right. But now, I just don't know. Maybe I'm not in love, maybe I just miss him." Sarah rubbed her forehead with her fingertips. "I feel like such an idiot."

"You said that already."

"You don't believe me?" Sarah grabbed her purse from beside her chair and withdrew something from it, then set it on the table. They both stared at it silently.

"What is it?" Libby asked.

"It's a bird that Sam Morgan carved. I stole it from his cabin before I left."

"Why?"

"Because I wanted an excuse. I wanted to know that if I got home and decided I needed to see him again, I'd have a reason to go back. I could return his little bird. I have the story all set up. The carving got mixed up with my stuff by accident." Sarah groaned and covered her face with her hands. "How desperate is that? I'm not that kind of woman. You know, the kind who manipulates and schemes to get herself a man."

"But it's a sensible plan," Libby commented. "I'm really proud of you for thinking of it."

Sarah pulled her hands away from her eyes. "How can you say that?"

"I'm just being practical. When you meet a man you love, sometimes you have to help things along a bit. I say use every advantage you have…that is, if you do love him."

"How can I love him?" Sarah asked. "I barely know him. I think mostly it's about lust and really great sex. You know what they say—women can't separate sex and love."

Libby nodded. "Why would you even want to do that?"

"If I give it a little time, I think everything will make sense. If it was just sex, then I'll forget about him and move on. And if it's really love, then I'll be miserable for the next five or six months. Or maybe for the rest of my life."

They ate their lunch in silence, Sarah mulling over all that had happened to her in the past couple of weeks. She'd tried so hard to put her feelings for Sam into words, and now they seemed to come out in a rush.

"I've been trying to figure out what it is about him that makes me want him so much. Because the truth is I know it's not just the sex. There's something more to it."

"What?"

Perhaps if she just kept talking, she would stumble upon it. And Libby was so good at asking questions and giving advice. Maybe she could figure it out. "When we were up on that mountain all alone, I always felt protected. Even when I was floundering around in the middle of a snowstorm, I knew instinctively that he would come to save me."

"Being able to trust and depend on a man is important," Libby said.

"But this is different. When I imagined the perfect man for me, I imagined a man who made a good living, who could provide well for a family, who respected me as his equal and who understood the demands of my career. But with Sam, it's different."

"How?"

"When we were on the mountain, everything came down to making sure we were safe and warm and well fed. I knew he was thinking about that all the time, so I didn't have to worry. He chopped the wood and he fetched the water and he built the fire and because of that, all was right for another day." Sarah paused. "He took me on a hike to see an old cabin and we stood inside this place, the log walls still standing and the roof long gone. And there, on the wooden mantel of the fireplace, some man had carved his initials and intertwined them with his wife's."

"How sweet," Libby said. "That's so romantic."

"But I didn't look at it that way. All I could think about was how this woman could have followed this man into the wilderness, leaving all she knew behind, family and friends, maybe a life that offered some luxuries. And at that moment, I knew if I had lived a hundred and fifty years ago and Sam had asked me to set out for the wilderness, I would have said 'yes.'" She stared at Libby, looking for answers in her friend's face. "Is that crazy? Or is that love?"

"Maybe," Libby said. "Or it could be…what do they call it? Natural selection?"

Sarah frowned, shaking her head. "What's that? You mean Darwin's theory?"

"Yes. Female animals gravitate toward the strongest of the pack since those are the males who will be able to provide in tough times. Sam is the alpha male."

"How do you know all this?"

A shout came from inside the house and a few minutes later, Libby's husband appeared on the verandah. Trey wore a finely tailored suit and silk tie and carried a roll of blueprints. "Hey there, Sarah. Welcome back." He bent over Libby and gave her a kiss, then rubbed her belly. "Hello, sweetheart. Hello, baby."

"Trey, what was the name of that show we were watching on PBS the other night? It was on right after my show, the one where I did the pit barbeque."

Trey's brow furrowed. "What show?"

"The one with the animals. It's all very simple," Libby explained, turning back to Sarah. "Trey said that's why I chose him, because he knew how to fix things around the house and I was living in a house that needed a lot of fixing."

"That's why you fell in love with Trey?" Sarah asked, glancing between the two of them.

"That and the great sex and a few other things. But when I saw him mowing the lawn that day and then wearing that tool belt, it was pretty much over for me."

"And you think I might be in love with Sam because he can chop wood?"

Libby nodded. "It's worth consideration, don't you think?"

"I don't know, Libby. It doesn't really make sense."

Trey chuckled. "Finally, the voice of reason."

"What good is chopping wood going to do here in Belfort? We have central heating and indoor plumbing. He can build me a log cabin but I already have a nice little house. And he can haul water from the river, but I have a faucet in my kitchen."

"It's not for me to figure out," Libby said with a shrug. "You're the one who's in love with him." She reached for her iced tea and took a slow sip. "Remember when Trey first came to town? You told me I wasn't going to find the man of my dreams unless I took a risk."

"You told her that?" Trey asked. He turned back to Libby. "Why didn't you ever tell me that?"

Libby raised her eyebrow and stared at Sarah from over the rim of her glass. "Perhaps you ought to listen to your own advice."

"You think I should go back?"

Libby picked up the carved bird and held it out to Sarah. "I think you always knew you would."

Sarah took the bird and held it in her hand, smoothing her thumb over the rough surface that Sam had carved. If she walked back into the wilderness for Sam, then she'd have to give up all the things that were most important in her life—her career, her best friend, her home. Would love be enough to make up for what she left behind? Or would she come to regret her decision?

Was this how that pioneer woman had felt all those years ago, making this choice between the man she loved and the life she knew? Sam had taught her to survive in the wilderness in case of emergency, but could she survive once she'd made the choice to join him there?

THE MIDSUMMER SUN hung low in the sky as Sam hiked up the last stretch to the cabin. He paused, massaging a cramp in his right leg. His cast had been removed three days ago and though his ankle was still weak, he'd decided to leave anyway. He'd made the entire climb in one day, determined to prove that he was still as strong as ever.

Carter had offered to bring him up on his ATV, but Sam had needed the hike, hoping it would give him a chance to regain some perspective on the last few months.

He'd tried to keep himself busy while he was in town, but he'd spent far too much time shooting pool and playing darts at the Lucky Penny. When he hadn't been there, he'd taken long drives in his truck, exploring back roads and thinking about the strange turn his life had taken.

What twist of fate had brought Sarah Cantrell into his life? Or had it been fate? If she hadn't read his articles in *Outdoor Adventure*, she might never have come looking for him. Maybe it wasn't fate, maybe it was journalism.

She'd come to him at the perfect time in his life, at the very moment when he'd found himself at a crossroads. One way took him back to the world he'd known, the other to a life of solitude in the mountains. She'd shown him what was still possible—happiness, contentment and love.

But after all that, he was back here, ready to spend another winter on his own. He'd waited for her to return to Sutter Gap, but she'd never even bothered to write. She'd obviously forgotten him the moment she'd returned to Belfort. She probably already had a bunch of new fish on the line.

Then again, maybe she thought *he'd* forgotten *her*. He'd made no attempt to contact her, waiting for her to make the first move. But what if she was doing the same thing?

As he stepped up to the front door, it suddenly swung open in front of him. He held his breath, half-expecting to see Sarah emerge, praying it might be her. In truth, he'd looked for her every day since she'd left, scanning the streets of Sutter Gap, even imagining that he'd seen her in the subway during a visit to New York City.

When Carter appeared from inside the cabin, Sam didn't hide his disappointment. "I see you're making yourself at home."

"Just wanted to be sure you got here in one piece."

"I know you didn't hike up here. You and I had breakfast together this morning in Sutter Gap."

"I brought the ATV up. I'm wearing down a real nice little path."

"I'm not sure I like that you can get up here in just a few hours. That anyone can get to me so easily."

Carter shrugged. "The world is gettin' smaller and smaller, Sam. Next thing you know there'll be a Blockbuster down by the creek and a shoppin' mall in the meadow."

"I sure hope not," Sam murmured, turning around to stare out over familiar territory.

Carter slapped him on the back. "Of course, by the time that comes to pass, you'll be long gone."

"I'm not going anywhere," Sam said. "In fact, I've been thinking about making some improvements. How hard do you think it would be to dig a well up here?"

"Don't you think you ought to check with the landlord before you do that?"

Sam frowned. "What are you saying?"

"I'm saying I think it's time you came down off this mountain, son. You've been up here for three years." He pointed to his chest. "Now, if you were an old guy like me, I could understand that and I wouldn't be stickin' my nose in where it don't belong. But you have a whole life ahead of you. You ought to be livin' it."

Sam shook his head. He couldn't disagree with Carter. Hell, he'd had some of the same thoughts himself over the past few months. Since he'd been forced to spend time in Sutter Gap, he'd come to realize that he liked being around people. It was nice to have breakfast with friends and see a movie occasionally, to take a hot shower every day and eat whatever he wanted.

The cabin had always been a refuge, but as he looked at it now, it seemed so austere and bleak, almost like a prison. Still, he'd made a life for himself here, a simple existence that made sense to him. It seemed easier to continue living that way than to think about going back to the hectic life he'd had.

"When me and the boys got back to your cabin after I took you down, Miz Cantrell was here. And I never saw a woman so worried over her man as she was. She questioned me for an hour, asking me to tell her everything you'd said and everything the paramedics had said. And when she got back to Sutter Gap the next morning, the first thing she wanted to know was where you were." He paused. "If I had a woman who cared about me that much, I wouldn't be hidin' out here."

"And what do you think I should do?" Sam asked.

"Go get her, boy," Carter suggested. "Quit wastin' time."

"She's not going to want to live here."

"Well, I expect not. But if a woman like that lets you into her life, you ought to be happy livin' anywhere. Instead of all lonely and sorry-lookin' up here. You're a smart boy. You'll figure a way to make it work."

"You know, being alone and being lonely are not the same thing," Sam said.

"No, they aren't. But if you spend much more time up here alone, you're gonna find out what lonely really is."

"Do you like telling me what to do?" Sam asked grumpily.

Carter shrugged. "Someone has to." He shook his head. "You never mentioned your pa, so I figured maybe he's not around anymore. And I don't have a boy of my own, so maybe I *am* stickin' my nose in where it don't belong. But I'm just statin' my opinion. You can take it or leave it."

Sam found himself chuckling softly. "Sometimes, I think Sarah Cantrell would have found a way into my life no matter where I was in this world. I could have been standing on a glacier in Greenland and I would have met her."

"Maybe." Carter grabbed a bucket from beside the door. "I'm goin' to get some water. Think about what I said."

Sam wandered inside the cabin. He didn't need to think about Sarah. Hell, from the moment she'd left Asheville, he'd been thinking of nothing else. That alone should be proof enough that he loved her. But Sam had never really had any experience with that emotion.

There had been women in his life, but he'd always managed to maintain a safe distance. And once they were gone, he'd simply moved on. So why couldn't he move on from Sarah? Sam sat down at the table and braced his head in his hands. He felt empty when he wasn't with her, as if a part of him was missing.

Building this cabin had been a good exercise, an experience that he'd never forget. He knew every notch in the logs, every piece of furniture in the room. He'd handled every stone used to build the fireplace.

As he stared over at the bed he'd made, Sam remembered the nights he'd spent there with Sarah. That had been an incredible experience, learning the soft curves of her body, discovering how to make her moan with pleasure. That was what he'd remember from this place.

Sam pushed back from the table and crossed to the bed, and then he grabbed his pillow and held it to his nose. Though he tried to discern her scent, it wasn't there anymore.

"It's got to be love," he muttered, "because if it isn't, then I'm in hell."

Sam looked around the cabin one last time. It wasn't right without her. "It's time to go," he said.

With a grin, he turned and walked back to the door, but at the last moment, he stopped. He ought to take at least one memento with him from his life here. The rest he would leave for the next occupant of the cabin.

But when he returned to the table, he couldn't find the little carved bird that Sarah had liked so much. He shrugged, then walked out the front door. Maybe it was better to leave it all behind.

A short time later, Carter reappeared with the bucket of water. Sam met him at the edge of the clearing and took the bucket from his hand. Then he tossed the water aside.

"I want you to take me back down the mountain," he said.

"You don't want to walk?"

Sam shook his head. "Nope, I want to get down as fast as I can. The cabin is yours along with everything in it. Enjoy it. It's time for me to move on."

Carter clapped him on the back. "All right. Let's get moving. We don't have much time to get back to the highway before it gets dark."

SARAH STARED at the columns of numbers on her laptop screen. She should have been excited to begin a new project, but *Bass Fishing Bonanza* was already turning into a disaster. Besides Billy Bob Barkley having all the charisma of a dead fish on camera, she'd had no luck convincing him to change the name of the show. And she'd had to wade through hours and hours of tape of Billy doing nothing but standing in his boat, casting his line into the water, and expounding on the excitement of fishing. It was simply excruciating.

"It's your own fault," she murmured. She'd been so convinced that the wilderness show would go forward that she'd made no contingency plans. Perhaps Libby's idea was worth considering. If she worked tirelessly for the next few months, she could probably put together a gardening show. She already had a host in mind and the show would be the perfect complement to Libby's *Southern Comforts* cooking show. Then she could toss Billy Bob back into the lake.

Sarah pushed away from the table and wandered over to the refrigerator. She grabbed a pitcher of lemonade and poured herself a glass, then set the pitcher on the counter. Strange how she'd just settled back into her life, never thinking twice about the conveniences she had—hot showers, an endless supply of drinking water, a refrigerator that made its own ice cubes. The list went on and on.

So how could she have been so happy living in Sam's cabin? "All you need is love," she murmured. The sentiment had seemed so silly to her, the idea that love could conquer all. But she and Sam had been content during those days they'd spent together. Though life had been a challenge, there was an elegant simplicity to living without the basic conveniences.

Sarah returned to the kitchen table and picked up

her BlackBerry. Her cell phone sat next to her computer. How many little appliances did she own? Hair dryer, curling iron, coffeemaker, vacuum cleaner, electric toothbrush. Every time she turned one on, she didn't even bother to appreciate how much simpler it made life.

She took a sip of her lemonade and sat down. Was she trying to convince herself she could live without electricity and running water? Or did this constant comparison of lifestyles have more to do with Sam? Over the past few months, she'd thought about what she'd left behind on that mountain, the possibilities that she'd ignored, the potential left unexplored.

She punched a key on her computer and her calendar popped up. The day was outlined in red and she stared at the note she'd made. "Three months," she murmured. It had been exactly three months since she'd left Sam in front of the hotel in Asheville.

She'd marked the date for a reason. Today, she was supposed to make a decision about the rest of her life. Today, she was supposed to decide once and for all, whether she loved Sam Morgan.

Sarah clicked on a document on her laptop and slowly read the text. She'd been working on the letter for a couple of weeks, but was no closer to finishing it. In truth, she wasn't even sure how she'd send it. Sam didn't have an address so perhaps writing it was a waste of time.

She clicked on another document and it opened onto the screen. She'd made the list late one night when she hadn't been able to sleep. A big plus sign headed the column on the right and a big minus sign hung over the column on the left.

She'd managed to find ninety-seven positives for

Sam Morgan, ranging from his beautiful blue eyes to his ability to make love in a bathtub. The negatives amounted to just three points—he lived on a mountain, in a cabin, without indoor plumbing. She'd listed his lack of a regular job on the positive side. The fact that he didn't have to get out of bed early in the morning to go to work was definitely a plus.

Objectively, he was the perfect man for her. So what was keeping her from making her move? Why wasn't she on her way to Sutter Gap this very morning? "Three months," she said. "You gave yourself three months." And in three months, her feelings for Sam hadn't changed. In truth, they'd gotten much stronger. But how did *he* feel?

Sarah had imagined the scene a hundred times before. She'd hike up to Sam's cabin and there he'd be, chopping wood or doing something that required no shirt. Her fantasy always seemed to have him in some state of undress. She'd profess her undying love for him in a tearful monologue. And then, she'd see it in his eyes—the uneasy look of a man who'd moved on.

Sarah quickly stood, shaking herself out of the daydream. This would have to stop! Sooner or later, she'd have to make a decision. She couldn't spend the rest of her life wondering what might have been. It either was or it wasn't and she needed to know. If she left now, she could be in Sutter Gap by dinnertime.

A strange sense of relief washed over her. Now that the decision was made, she felt good. No matter what happened, good or bad, she'd be able to handle it.

With that, Sarah raced upstairs to pack. But halfway up the stairs, the doorbell rang.

She stopped cold. She'd promised Libby a trip into Charleston to shop for baby supplies. The newest Marbury was due in just a month and Libby had called last night, frantic because, according to a baby magazine she was reading, she didn't have enough receiving blankets.

After shopping, they planned to have lunch at Libby's favorite restaurant and then stop by the station to meet with the new floor director for Libby's show.

But Libby would understand. And the floor director would just have to wait. Sarah hurried back through the front hall to the door. When she opened it, she found her friend standing on the porch, holding a ball of string.

She handed it to Sarah as she rushed inside. "I have to use your bathroom. Gosh, I can't go fifteen minutes without having to pee. If this baby gets any bigger inside of me, I might as well just live in the bathroom."

"What's this for?" Sarah asked, following her along the way to the powder room just off the kitchen. "Oh, wait, let me guess. We're going to do that thing where you hang the string over your belly and it tells you whether you're having a boy or a girl."

"I'm having a boy," Libby said.

Sarah gasped. "You are? Why didn't you tell me?"

"We've known for ages. I figured I better tell you now or you'd hear from someone else. Trey let it slip to the Thockmorton sisters yesterday so it'll be all over the county by suppertime tonight."

Sarah grabbed Libby and gave her a fierce hug. "I'm so happy for you. And I have something very important to tell you."

"That's great, but I have to go." Libby hurried into the powder room.

"So what's the string for?" Sarah called through the door.

"It's yours. It was sitting on the porch, in front of your door."

Frowning, Sarah examined the tightly wound ball. "It's not mine. I've never seen it before." She shrugged. "Maybe one of the neighborhood kids left it there."

A few minutes later, Libby stepped out of the powder room, looking far less frazzled. She ran her fingers through her pale hair. "Let's go. It's a forty-five minute drive to Charleston. If you drive fast, we'll only have to stop once."

"About shopping…" Sarah began. "I was hoping we might be able to do it another day. I've got something really important I need to do."

Libby frowned. "What could possibly be more important than following your best friend around while she obsesses over receiving blankets?"

Sarah laughed, then drew Libby into another hug. "I think I need to go find Sam. It's time I let him know how I feel."

Libby stepped back, a wide smile on her face, her eyes brimming with tears.

"Oh, don't cry," Sarah said. "It's all good. I love him and I'm planning to tell him that."

"I guess lunch can wait," Libby said, waving her hand in front of her eyes to dry her tears. "It's the hormones. Really, I'm very happy for you."

Sarah slipped her arm through Libby's and led her to the door. They pushed open the screen door and stepped outside onto the porch, then walked down the front steps.

"You have to promise you'll call me and let me know what happens," Libby insisted.

Sarah nodded. "I will. Wish me luck."

"Good luck," Libby said.

She turned to walk back to the house, but then noticed a huge pile of brush in the middle of her lawn. "What is that?" she said, pointing at the pile.

Libby stopped. "It's a pile of sticks and leaves."

"I can see that," Sarah said. "But who put it there?"

She crossed the lawn, curious as to how such a mess could have been made on her front lawn without her even noticing. As she came closer, Sarah realized that the mess wasn't just leaves and sticks. It was a debris shelter.

Libby joined her, peering into the small opening. "Is there an animal in there? Maybe it's a little raccoon house."

"It's a debris shelter," Sarah explained, bending over to look inside.

"A what?"

"A survival shelter. You build it in the woods to protect yourself from the elements."

As she slowly straightened, Sarah was almost afraid to believe. She drew a ragged breath then glanced up and down the street. Her breath caught in her throat when she saw Sam's truck parked across from her house.

And then Sarah saw him, standing on the other side of the truck, his arms resting on the hood, his gaze fixed on her. "Oh!" She pressed her hand to her chest and felt her heart hammering inside. Her knees suddenly went weak and she couldn't seem to move.

Libby was still staring at the debris shelter. "I can

call Trey and he'll come over tonight and clean this up for you."

"No, it's fine," Sarah whispered.

Libby turned to look at her, then followed Sarah's gaze across the street. She glanced back and forth, then slowly smiled. "Is that him?"

"Then there *is* a man standing next to that truck?" Sarah asked. "I'm not just imagining it?"

Libby nodded. "There is. He's wearing jeans and a blue T-shirt. And he's quite handsome."

"What's he doing here?"

"Why don't you stop standing there like a ninny and go ask?" Libby suggested.

"I don't know what to say."

"Just tell him what you told me."

"I can't remember what I told you."

"Sarah, I don't think you'd be getting this flustered if you didn't have serious feelings for this guy. Take a risk. Cross the street and find out what he wants. Just look both ways before you cross. You wouldn't want to get hit by a bus just moments before you profess your love for the most perfect man in the world." She gave Sarah a little push. "As for me, I'm just going to drive on down to the Tastee Freeze and have a hot-fudge sundae. Call me later and let me know how it went." She hurried down the walk to her car, then waved at both Sarah and Sam before she got inside and drove away.

Slowly, Sarah approached the street. Sam waited for her, his gaze fixed on her face, a tiny smile playing at his lips.

"What are you doing here?" Sarah asked.

"I was just in the neighborhood." He stepped out from behind the truck and Sarah noticed that his cast was gone. He carried a familiar black suitcase. "I found this alongside the trail. I think it's yours."

"It's been a while," she said.

"Exactly three months," he said. "God, it's good to see you, Sarah."

"And you," she replied.

"I see you got my gift."

She frowned, then glanced down, surprised to see the ball of string still clutched in her palm. "This was from you? I don't understand."

"You will," he said. He took her hand and led her back to the porch, then sat them both down on the steps. He stared out at the street. "This is a nice town."

Sarah watched him, unable to read his mood. "Thank you."

"Different than Sutter Gap," he commented.

"Very different."

A long silence grew between them and Sarah felt her nerves begin to fray. She drew a deep breath. Now was her chance to tell him exactly how she felt. "Take the risk," she muttered.

"What?" Sam said, his head snapping around to look at her.

"Sam, I have something I have to tell you and—"

He held up his hand to stop her. "Just give me a few more seconds," he said. "I know what I want to say but I just have to figure out how to say it."

Sarah nodded, a sick feeling twisting at her stomach. This wasn't going to go well. From the uneasy look on his face, he was about to deliver bad news. And she didn't want to hear it. She scrambled to her feet, dropping the ball of string. It rolled down the front steps and Sam reached out to grab it.

He stood and turned to her. "When we first met, I was looking for no strings. I thought that if I just avoided any kind of emotional attachment, I'd never be hurt again. I'd decided I was going to go through life all alone and I was fine with that—until you came along and messed up my plan."

"What are you saying?" Sarah asked.

"Tie me up," Sam said, holding out the ball. "I want the strings. I want to know you're thinking of me when I'm not around and I want to know you're happy to be with me when I am around. I want to know that fifty years from now, I can still look into those beautiful green eyes of yours and see the woman who hiked up a mountainside to save me." He reached out and cupped her face in his hands. "I love you, Sarah. I'm not afraid to say it because it's true. And I don't care if you're not sure about your own feelings, because I'm planning to stick around here until you are."

Sarah blinked, unable to believe what she'd heard. All her life, she'd been running from this, determined to shield her heart from any kind of pain or rejection. But in a single instant, she realized that she hadn't really been running. She'd just been waiting, for a man like Sam to walk into her life. "You want to live here?" Sarah asked.

Sam pointed to the debris shelter. "I'm all set. I thought I'd just hang out here on your front lawn until you invited me inside." He smiled crookedly. "So what do you say? Do you think we can make this work?"

Sarah gazed into his eyes. How could she ever have questioned her feelings? Everything was so clear now. She reached out and ran her finger along his bottom lip. "I love you, Sam. It took me a while to figure that out, but now that I have, I don't have any doubts."

With a wild whoop, Sam grabbed her and picked her up off her feet. Sarah wrapped her legs around his waist and lost herself in a long, deep kiss. The taste of his mouth, the smell of his hair, the sound of his voice, everything about him filled her with sheer joy. This was the man she loved and he'd be hers for the rest of her life.

Sam carried her up the front steps, then opened the door and stepped inside.

"What about the cabin?"

"It's there if we ever want to go back again. But I'm ready to make a life wherever you are, Sarah. *Outdoor Adventure* has offered me a job writing for them. And they've had a bunch of calls from publishers interested in a book of my stories. And there's this crazy woman who wants to make a television show about my experiences in the woods."

Sarah frowned. "I knew those reality people were going to get to you. How could you even—"

Sam pressed his finger to her lips. "I was talking about you. And if the offer is still good, I'd like to do it. We could use that piece of land that I have. It's close to Sutter Gap and right off the highway."

"The offer is still good," Sarah said.

Sam bent closer and brushed a kiss across her lips. "Then I guess I'm going to have to start calling you boss. Is there anything I can do for you now, boss?"

"There is one thing," Sarah said, running her hands through his hair.

"What's that?" Sam asked, his voice low and husky.

She nuzzled her face in the curve of his neck, kissing a spot just below his ear. "I could really use a bath," she whispered.

1

JO BETH SIGHED and tried to be content, too, but she was still restless. Still edgy. Still agitated and dissatisfied and riled up. And it wasn't *all* because of the three hands who'd quit on her to follow the summer rodeo circuit, leaving her shorthanded when she needed them most, or the half-dozen city slickers who were due to invade the Diamond J in less than a week, or her best friend's wedding at which she had agreed to be—God help her—the maid of honor. It wasn't even the bookkeeping.

It was that damned Clay Madison!

If she'd been getting laid regularly, it wouldn't be so bad. But it had been over six months since that weekend in Dallas with Jim, the cattle broker, and she'd gone without for four months before that. It'd been so long, she'd almost forgotten what it was she was missing. And then Clay Madison had swaggered onto the scene with that lazy, loose-hipped, loose-kneed cowboy saunter of his and had reminded her of *exactly* what she was doing without. She'd have avoided him if she could have, but he was best man to her maid of honor, so ignoring him wasn't an option.

Unfortunately, having sex with him wasn't, either.

Jo Beth had two ironclad rules when it came to

sex. She didn't do it close to home. And she didn't do cowboys. Ever.

And, hell, it wasn't as if Clay had ever looked twice at her, anyway. She wasn't the kind of woman a man like him looked at, or even took any particular notice of. She had a decent body—a bit on the skinny side, true, but decent, nonetheless—and she had a nice enough face. Nothing that would stop traffic, but it didn't stop clocks, either. She freely admitted she didn't have enough feminine graces to be what anyone would call beautiful, but she had a certain lean and rangy wholesomeness going for her, an outdoorsy girl-next-door kind of thing that wasn't *completely* unappealing.

Except to men like Clay Madison.

Men like Clay Madison didn't want the wholesome girl-next-door. They wanted flash and sparkle in their women. They wanted curvy bodies, big hair, fluttering eyelashes and glossy wet-lipped smiles. They wanted adoring, tractable, bosomy, bubble-brained buckle bunnies who gave head at the drop of a trophy belt buckle and didn't make a fuss when the party was over. And they got them. By the truckload. In every town and every city where the rodeo played, the buckle bunnies lined up, waiting for some cowboy to give them a tumble. And if that cowboy happened to be a handsome-as-sin, four-time pro-rodeo bull-riding champion with shoulders a yard wide, a tight little butt and a wicked gleam in his soulful brown eyes, well, that cowboy inevitably got first pick. And it was for certain he would never pick a woman like her.

Not that she'd pick him, either. Not for anything real or permanent. But she sure as hell wouldn't mind having him in her bed. Just once. Just one time to see if he was as good as he looked.

"And, damn, I bet he's fine," she murmured, her eyes drifting closed to better imagine just how it would be...

If you enjoyed what you just read,
then we've got an offer you can't resist!

Take 2 bestselling love stories FREE!

Plus get a FREE surprise gift!

Clip this page and mail it to Harlequin Reader Service®

IN U.S.A.	IN CANADA
3010 Walden Ave.	P.O. Box 609
P.O. Box 1867	Fort Erie, Ontario
Buffalo, N.Y. 14240-1867	L2A 5X3

YES! Please send me 2 free Harlequin Temptation® novels and my free surprise gift. After receiving them, if I don't wish to receive anymore, I can return the shipping statement marked cancel. If I don't cancel, I will receive 4 brand-new novels each month, before they're available in stores. In the U.S.A., bill me at the bargain price of $3.80 plus 25¢ shipping and handling per book and applicable sales tax, if any*. In Canada, bill me at the bargain price of $4.47 plus 25¢ shipping and handling per book and applicable taxes**. That's the complete price and a savings of 10% off the cover prices—what a great deal! I understand that accepting the 2 free books and gift places me under no obligation ever to buy any books. I can always return a shipment and cancel at any time. Even if I never buy another book from Harlequin, the 2 free books and gift are mine to keep forever.

142 HDN DZ7U
342 HDN DZ7V

Name   (PLEASE PRINT)

Address   Apt.#

City   State/Prov.   Zip/Postal Code

Not valid to current Harlequin Temptation® subscribers.

Want to try two free books from another series?
Call 1-800-873-8635 or visit www.morefreebooks.com.

* Terms and prices subject to change without notice. Sales tax applicable in N.Y.
** Canadian residents will be charged applicable provincial taxes and GST.
    All orders subject to approval. Offer limited to one per household.
    ® are registered trademarks owned and used by the trademark owner and or its licensee.

TEMP04R   ©2004 Harlequin Enterprises Limited

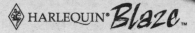

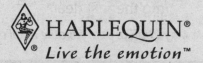